The Ninth Jewel
of the Mughal Crown

The Ninth Jewel of the Mughal Crown

The Birbal Tales
from the Oral Traditions of India

Written and Illustrated
by James Moseley

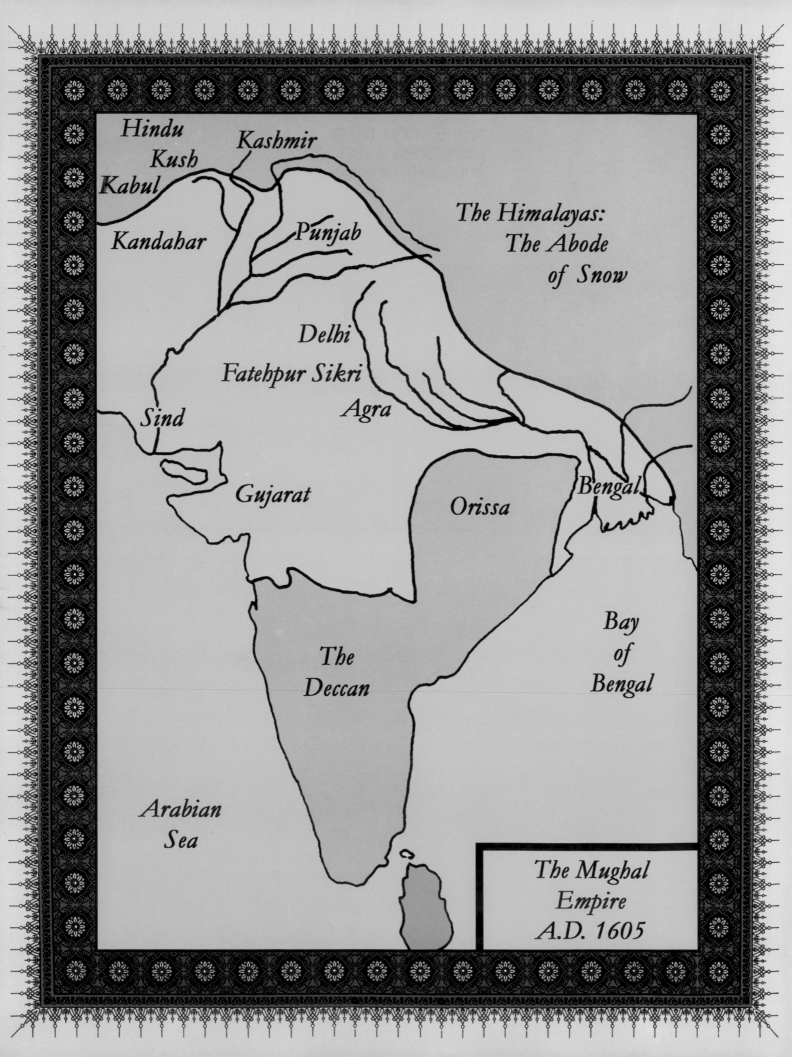

Hindu
Kush

Kabul

Kashmir

Kandahar

Punjab

The Himalayas:
The Abode
of Snow

Delhi

Fatehpur Sikri

Agra

Sind

Gujarat

Orissa

Bengal

The
Deccan

Bay
of
Bengal

Arabian
Sea

The Mughal
Empire
A.D. 1605

Table of Contents

Cover and Interior Design: Peri Poloni, Knockout Design
www.knockoutbooks.com

For information address the publisher:

Printed in China

Summerwind Marketing, Inc.
P.O. Box 60013
Pasadena CA 91116-6013
(888) 820-8140
jimmoseley@wwdb.org
www.birbal.net

Library of Congress Cataloging in Publication Data

Moseley, James
        The Ninth Jewel of the Mughal Crown:
                The Birbal Tales from the Oral Traditions of India
        Fiction
        LC Control Number 00 092689

ISBN 0-9704447-1-0
First Edition

To Madlene, Natalie, Christopher,
Jamie, and Sasha

And

To Mom and Dad

The Ninth Jewel

VERY LONG AGO AND FAR AWAY, the Great Mughal Emperor of India died, leaving Throne and Crown to a thirteen-year-old Prince, named Akbar.

Bold and intelligent, the boy had to battle fierce enemies to defend the vast kingdom that his father had left him.

But when peace at last shone across his beautiful dominions, Akbar brought to India a Golden Age.

The young King allowed all people to worship in their own ways. Subjects of every color and tongue stood equal before his Throne. Akbar loved poetry, painting, and architecture, and he brought the wisest and most talented men he could find to the Imperial Court.

Nine of these exceptional men were so gifted, so rare, people called them *"Nava Ratna* — The Nine Jewels of the Mughal Crown"* — for their value was above rubies.

One of them, Tansen, was a singer so skilled that candles burst into flame at the mystical power of his song.

Another, Daswant, was a painter who became First Master of the Age.

Todar Mal was a financial wizard.

Abul Fazl was a great historian, whose brother, Faizi, was a famed poet.

Abud us-Samad was a brilliant calligrapher and designer of Imperial coins.

Man Singh was a mighty general.

Mir Fathullah Shirazi was a financier, philosopher, physician and astronomer.

But of all Akbar's Nine Jewels, the people's favorite was his Minister – or Raja[1]—Birbal: the clever, the generous, and the just.

---

[1] Ministers at Akbar's court were called rajas, or kings, to give greater glory to the Emperor, who was styled Shah-in-shah, or King of kings.

How Akbar Met Birbal

BIRBAL, WHOSE NAME MEANS "strong, brave warrior," was actually born with the name of Mahesh Das. He was still a young boy living in the country when the tinkling of horse bells, the thunder of hooves, and the flash of magnificent turbans signaled the approach of a Royal hunting party.

Akbar, who was a very young King and loved sport, had ridden long and hard with his companions without finding any game. Seeing the skinny lad by the wayside, the Emperor called out:

"Is there a village nearby, little man, where we can water our horses?"

Mahesh looked at the elegant cavalcade fearlessly and said:

"At our house we have a tank full of fresh, cool water..."

Akbar swept the boy up behind his saddle, and all galloped away in the direction Mahesh pointed out.

The little boy drew water for the horsemen with great courtesy and speed. The King was impressed. When his turn came to drink, Akbar took the bowl from Mahesh's little brown hands and, looking straight into his eyes, asked:

"What is your name?"

"What is your name?" smiled Mahesh. "If you can tell me that, you deserve to learn my name."

Akbar dropped the bowl, and the fresh water vanished into the thirsty dust. Nobody dared to speak to the Emperor that way.

"Do you know who I am?" spluttered Akbar.

"Yes," said Mahesh mildly. "But I'll wager you do not know the name of the Brahmin in our village. So where is the greatness of kings?"

The noblemen sucked in their breath with horror. They looked expectantly at Akbar, and he scowled back at them. Then the Emperor's gaze met the shining black eyes and half-smile of the tiny country lad...and all he could do was laugh.

"Little man, you are right to remind a king that he should not be proud. I see you have a bold heart and a wise mind. Here."

He took a costly ring from his hand and gave it to the boy.

"When you are grown, present yourself, with this ring, at my Court. I will remember you, little brother."

And, leaving the boy to ponder the wonderful ring, the Imperial hunting party cantered off.

Mahesh Das Seeks His Fortune

WHEN MAHESH DAS became a young man, he took the few coins that were all his savings, along with the royal ring, kissed his mother farewell, and set out upon the long road to the great new capital of the Empire, Fatehpur Sikri.

Never in his country childhood had he imagined so many people as he found in this splendid city. Mountains of sweets, colored golden, green, and red, were sold in the bazaar, along with precious silks, elegant lambswool hats, and gold jewelry hammered as thin and fine as a feather. Mahesh was amazed. He felt as though he could wind through the covered alleys and wide streets for months and never see the same thing twice.

Huge camels glided past, water-sellers gave their nasal cries, acrobats and magicians attracted small crowds, incense spiraled from the many temples, and then, as if from nowhere, the haunting notes of a flute wandered above the moving crowd. It was all Mahesh could do to keep his mind upon the purpose of his journey. He pushed on to the massive, red walls of the Palace.

The palace gate was so vast and so ornate, Mahesh thought it must be the door to the Emperor's own home. But it was far from that. Beautiful as it was, it was merely the outermost edge of the great city within a city that was the Imperial Court.

As soon as the guard on duty noticed the astonished gaze of this simple-looking country lad, he slashed the air with his spear and barred Mahesh's path.

"Where do you think you're going, oaf?"

"I have come to see the King," said Mahesh, mildly.

"Oh, have you?" sneered the guard. "Why, how very fortunate. His Majesty has been wondering when you'd come..."

"Yes, I know," said Mahesh. "Well, now I'm here."

"Fool! Do you think Shah Akbar has time to waste with ignorant yokels? Go away!"

Mahesh looked at the quivering mustaches of this arrogant warrior and half smiled.

"Please, uncle. When you were younger, no doubt you fought wonderfully on the Emperor's frontiers. Now that they have given you this easy job — why do you want to risk it?"

The guard's jaw dropped.

"Why you impudent worm! I'll lop off your head at a single

...I'll...I'll..."

But he stopped short as Mahesh held out Akbar's ring. Even a guard could recognize the Imperial Seal.

"Many years ago," said Mahesh, "our good King sent for me. Now let me pass."

Annoyed, the guard saw he would have to admit the lad. But he was unwilling to let him go in for free.

"You can pass on one condition," he scowled. "If you obtain anything from the Emperor, you will give half to me."

"Agreed," smiled Mahesh, and entered.

Shade trees rocked with the breeze as Mahesh followed the path through the royal gardens. Cooling fountains murmured, and the perfume of roses coiled like an invisible serpent through the air.

Each building he passed seemed more magnificent than the last. Finally, he recognized that a pavilion of shimmering marble, with a forest of columns and fretted arches, must be the Hall of Public Audience. So many richly dressed courtiers thronged there that he felt any one of them might turn out to be the King. But at last he saw, seated upon a throne of gold that was studded with flashing gems, a man of simple elegance, whose nobility glistened in his eyes. Mahesh knew. This was Akbar.

Sliding past Uzbek generals, Rajput princes, and Persian artists, Mahesh bowed before the Throne and said:

"May your shadow never grow less, O Full Moon!"

Akbar smiled.

"Ask a favor, O One of Bright Prospects."

"Your Majesty," said Mahesh, rising. "I have come at your command, which none dare disobey." And he handed the Emperor the ring that Akbar had given the country boy so many years ago.

The King laughed with pleasure.

"Welcome, welcome! What can I do for you? What can I give you? What is your heart's desire?"

The courtiers hushed at this unusually generous reception by the King. Who was this shabby-looking young man?

Mahesh thought for a moment and then said evenly:

"I would like you to punish me with one hundred lashes."

You could have heard a pin drop upon the gleaming marble floor.

"What!" exploded the king. "A hundred lashes? But you have done nothing wrong!"

"Will Your Majesty go back on his promise to fulfill my heart's desire?"

"Well, no...a King must always keep his word..."

So, with great reluctance, Akbar ordered Mahesh's back to be stripped. Then he commanded the Court Executioner to lay a hundred lashes of the whip across his nut-brown shoulders. To the acute interest of all the assembled courtiers, Mahesh endured every stroke with a stony expression and without uttering a sound.

But when the whip had cracked for the fiftieth time, Mahesh suddenly jumped up and shouted: "Stop!"

"Ah!" cried Akbar. "Then you see how foolish you are being..."

"No, Sire. It is only that when I came here to see you, I was unable to enter the Palace unless I promised the guard at the front gate half of whatever the King's generosity would get me. So I have taken my half of the hundred lashes. Please be kind enough to deliver the rest of them to your guard."

The entire crowd shouted with laughter, and Akbar loudest of all. His fingers snapped, and in less time than it takes to tell, the unhappy guard was hauled into the Presence Chamber to receive his humiliating "bribe."

When he was dragged out in disgrace, Akbar turned to Mahesh and said:

"You are as brave as when you were a child, and, if possible, you have grown even cleverer. I have tried in many ways to weed out corruption at my Court, but your little trick today will do more to make greedy officials honest than if I passed a thousand laws. From now on, since your wit is mightier than a warrior's sword, you shall be called 'Birbal.' And you shall stay by my side and advise me in all things."

The Justice Bell

SHORTLY BEFORE BIRBAL'S ARRIVAL, Akbar had moved his Court from Agra to the elegant new city of Fatehpur Sikri. He did this to be near the tomb of his mentor, Shaikh Salim Chishti, who had recently died.

Akbar wanted to choose a new Judge for his new city, but without Shaikh Salim to advise him, the King's Council was taking some time to suggest a person suitably wise and honest for the post.

In the meantime, Akbar decided to hang a bell outside his private apartments in the Palace, with a rope dangling from his high verandah to the courtyard below. That way, if any citizens had been wronged, they could simply jingle the bell. Then the Emperor would lean out, hear their problem, and pass his judgment on the spot.

One day, at about noon, the bell sounded.

"What now?" growled Akbar, rising from the food that the harem servants had just placed before him.

But when he leaned out of the window and looked below, there was no one to be seen.

"Must have been the wind," thought Akbar, returning to his table.

But no sooner had he seated himself than the bell jangled again.

"Just a minute," he said, jumping up. But, as before, there was not a soul to be seen. The Emperor looked suspiciously at the bell, rang it once or twice, shrugged and started back to his lunch.

"If it is somebody's idea of a joke," he said darkly, "he will soon learn how hard it is to amuse a hungry king..."

Hardly had these words escaped his lips when the bell tingled again. Quick as a flash, the Emperor bounded to the balcony, just in time to see an old bullock, nothing but skin and bones, gnawing at the bell rope, far below. Throwing his head back, Akbar laughed.

"Send Birbal to ask what the bullock wants," he commanded one of his servants. "After all, no subject shall ring the Justice Bell in vain!"

Birbal led the old animal to the stables and gave it hay. Then he made inquiries until its owner was found. He was a very old farmer with two sons. The next day, farmer, sons, and bullock were brought into the Imperial Presence.

"Is this your bullock?" asked Akbar.

"Yes, *Maharaj* [2]," stammered the old farmer.

"Why do you let it roam free near the Palace?"

"I did not know it would bother Your Majesty...but it is old and feeble,

[2] "Great king."

≪ 24 ≫

and we can no longer afford to feed it. So we have sent it away."

Now Birbal turned to the man's two sons:

"Does your father still work in the fields?"

"No," said one. "He is rather old for that these days."

"Then, Your Majesty, in accordance with the bullock's plea for justice by ringing the bell, I recommend that you send the bullock and the farmer into exile together."

"So be it," said Akbar, smiling.

"But, Sire!" protested the old man. "How can I survive alone in the world at my time of life?"

"*Jahanpanah* [3]," said the sons, "our father has worked hard in our fields all his life to give us a home. Please do not force us to abandon him in his old age."

Birbal said:

"Has not this bullock served you faithfully in the fields all its life? And do you not drive it away now that it is too weak and old to work?"

The three farmers hung their heads.

"It is your duty," pronounced the King, "to care for this faithful animal until its death."

The old man thought for a moment, and then promised:

"Yes, Sire. With all my heart."

[3] "One who seizes the world," a title of respect given only to the Mughal Emperor.

Birbal The Judge

THE KING'S COUNCIL was still arguing about who should become the new Judge. Of course every counselor proposed one of his own relatives. That way he could count on a lenient sentence if ever he got in trouble — and considerable bribe money for influencing the sentences of others.

But Akbar began to consider Birbal for the post. The King was convinced that he was intelligent enough; but there would be tremendous opposition among the nobles. Even the Queen was upset.

"How do you expect people to listen to this 'Birbal,' as you call him? Will a Prince of the Royal House accept the judgment of a poor Brahmin from a dirty village no one ever has heard of?"

"They will accept what I command them to accept," said Akbar. "But don't you see how clever he is? I think he would make an excellent judge."

"Hmf," said the *Begam*[4] with her nose in the air. "If you are willing to appoint a layman to this exalted position, I cannot understand why you pass over your own brother-in-law!"

Akbar winced.

"Your brother?" he asked, lamely.

"What is wrong with my brother?" snapped the Queen. "Is he not a high-born Rajput Prince?"

"Jai Mal is a good warrior," said Akbar slowly.

"A superb warrior," corrected the Queen.

"Yes, of course," said Akbar. "But has he quite got that — that wisdom that a judge requires?"

"Put him to the test," said the *Begam*, proudly. "You will soon forget this 'Birbal' fellow you dragged in from a hunt when you see the dazzling qualities your own brother-in-law possesses!"

Akbar smiled. The Queen was never more beautiful than when anger gave luster to her Rajput pride.

The Emperor commanded Jai Mal and Birbal to appear before him. To the astonishment of his counselors, Akbar announced that one of them soon would become the new Judge of Fatehpur Sikri.

To find out which was better suited to the job, Akbar would present three cases to the two men. The one who solved the cases, or handed down the fairer sentence, would receive the judge's mantle.

Jai Mal smiled and turned his head slightly to the marble fretwork screen above the Audience Hall. Behind this, the Queen could watch

_____
[4] "Queen" or "Lady"

all Court proceedings without being seen. Her brother nodded as he caught her glistening eye — and without raising his head, Birbal noticed this, too.

And the Emperor summoned the first case.

The First Case: The Mango Tree

TWO MEN CAME into the Imperial Presence: Shankar and Ramu. Both were small farmers.

"You have appealed for justice to the Crown," said Akbar gravely. "State your complaints."

Shankar spoke up fearlessly.

"*Maharaj*, there is a mango tree between our two farms and this man pretends that all the fruit is his, even though I have watered that tree since it was a sapling."

"How do you answer that?" Birbal asked the trembling old Ramu.

"Master," began Ramu in a frail thread of a voice. "I planted that tree on the day my first son was born. I have cared for it these thirty years. Now this man, Shankar, takes all the fruit he wants and even sells it."

Akbar rubbed his chin.

"Jai Mal, what is your verdict?"

Jai Mal was impatient with these farmers' affairs.

"I honestly believe these two men should be whipped and driven from the Court for wasting Your Majesty's precious time. There is no way to tell from looking at a tree who planted it. And besides, how many mangoes can either of them eat?"

The courtiers joined Jai Mal in laughter. But Akbar did not laugh, and the merriment died suddenly on their lips.

"Birbal, what do you propose?"

"I would like to have the court adjourn," said Birbal quietly.

"What, more delay?" chided Jai Mal.

"So be it," commanded the Emperor, and the two farmers were sent home.

That night, Birbal disguised himself as a villager and made his way to Shankar's house. Pounding on the door he cried out:

"Shankar! Shankar! Thieves are stealing your mangoes!"

It was late at night, and there was no answer. Birbal pounded the door again. At last, without even opening the door, Shankar's angry voice came from within:

"Go away, you fool! Do you think I am going to fight with thieves in the middle of the night over a few rotten mangoes? Let a man sleep in peace!"

Birbal smiled. Then he continued to the hut of Ramu. Knocking on his door he cried:

"Ramu! Ramu! Thieves are running away with the mangoes on the tree!"

"Eh?" shouted the old man inside. "Wife! Did you hear that? Get me my stick! Get me my knife! Now we have not only to defend our mango tree from that greedy neighbor, but from thieves as well! But I have planted it with my own hands, and it is almost like a child to me. Hurry, wife! My sandals!"

And so, not even seeing Birbal in the dark, Ramu ran off toward the mango tree.

Even when Ramu saw no sign of thieves, Birbal saw that he climbed up into the tree and prepared to spend the whole night on a limb, guarding the fruit in case the thieves should return. Chuckling at Ramu's bravery, Birbal went home to his own, comfortable bed.

The next morning, an exhausted Ramu and a confident Shankar again presented themselves at Court.

"Well?" asked Akbar.

Birbal stepped forward.

"I have not been able to decide who owns the tree," he began.

The courtiers howled. Jai Mal smiled. And behind the marble screen the beautiful *Begam* rubbed her hands in glee.

Birbal held up his hand for silence.

"But here is what I propose. All the mangoes shall be gathered from the tree and divided equally between Ramu and Shankar. Then the tree itself shall be cut and splintered, and that, too, shall be divided between them, as firewood."

Jai Mal shot a black look at Birbal. Why hadn't he thought of that?

Shankar was the first to speak:

"You are wise and fair, Birbal Sahib. I agree to this."

But Ramu was silent. Akbar leaned forward.

"Does this judgment please you, father?" asked the King.

"No, Sire," said Ramu. "I have tended that tree for over half my life. It has fed my family, shaded us after many a weary day's work in the fields, and given shelter to a thousand birds, who have brought music into our simple lives. I cannot see it cut down. Please, *Maharaj*, you may give my tree to Shankar."

You could have heard a cricket sing, for the entire Court now realized the truth. At last Birbal spoke:

"My sentence," he said, "is thirty lashes for Shankar, or let him pay thirty silver rupees to his honest neighbor, for it is to the Emperor himself that he has told this lie."

Akbar nodded and clapped his hands:

"Next case!"

The Second Case: The False Mother

NOW, TWO WOMEN approached the Throne, presenting a baby to the King. Each woman claimed that the infant was her own. Each woman said that the other had stolen the baby from her. Both pleaded hysterically, shedding real tears and pulling their hair. It was hard to see which was lying.

Akbar turned to his brother-in-law:

"Jai Mal, how will you solve this case?"

Jai Mal thought a moment. Remembering the case of the mango tree, he decided to test the women in the same way.

"Have the child cut in two. Give half to each woman. That should end the quarrel."

But instead of behaving differently, as Jai Mal hoped, both women reacted exactly the same. Falling at the feet of the

Emperor, they wailed for mercy. Their anguished sobs gave no clue as to which might be the real mother. Behind her screen the *Begam* turned her head away in shame.

Akbar turned to Birbal:

"Will you try this difficult case?"

Without a moment's hesitation, Birbal said:

"Let a servant bring a glass of poisoned buttermilk."

Both the hysterical women were stunned into silence. Only the cooing of the baby could be heard in the vaulted marble hall.
Birbal whispered instructions to the servant. When he came back with a jewel-encrusted cup, Birbal handed it to one of the women.

"Give this poison to the child," he ordered, "or you shall drink it yourself."

The woman froze in terror. She looked at the Emperor, but there was no sign that he would contradict Birbal's cruel command. Seeing no hope, she cradled the baby and murmured a prayer as she raised the glass to the infant's lips.

"No!" cried the other woman, and, darting forward, she snatched the cup, raised it to her own lips, and drained it to the last drop.

With a clang, the cup fell from her trembling hands to the marble floor. The court gasped as she sank to her knees, sobbing. The Emperor rose from his throne. But before he could reach the woman, Birbal was at her side, raising her up and saying:

"Only a true mother would make that sacrifice to save her child. There was no poison in the drink. Your baby is restored to you forever."

The courtiers roared their approval.

Jai Mal clenched his fists.

And Akbar clapped his hands:

"Next case!"

The Third Case: The Shape of a Diamond

TWO RESPECTABLE MERCHANTS and four other men came before the Throne. Dhanlal was the first of them to speak:

"O Peacock of the Age, I am well known as a wealthy jeweler in the bazaar. Last night I invited this man, Prakash, to dine at my house. As he is also a jeweler and a member of my caste, I did not think he would steal from me. But in the presence of these four men, who were also my honored guests, he handled and admired a huge diamond, which I recently purchased. This morning when I searched my house, the diamond was nowhere to be found. I am charging Prakash with theft."

"Just a moment," interrupted Jai Mal, hoping to get ahead of Birbal. "How do you know your other guests did not steal it?"

"Because," answered Dhanlal, "they are all honest men.

They all agree to what they saw, while Prakash here will not admit that I even showed him a diamond."

"But he didn't!" shouted Prakash. "This man is a notorious cheat! He gets money from people by charging them with crimes they didn't commit. I never saw a diamond in his house, and these men didn't, either. They are just hired liars, that's all."

"Silence!" thundered Jai Mal. "You have no witnesses at all, so it is your word against five. I find you guilty."

"Birbal?" asked Akbar leaning back in his throne.

Birbal rubbed his chin a moment and then turned to the witnesses.

"All of you saw the diamond in Prakash's hand?"

"He was sitting at the table right next to me, drooling over it," said the first witness.

"He said it was one of the finest stones he had ever seen," said the second witness.

"He said it would fetch a fortune at the Palace," said the third witness.

"And he even said such a jewel could corrupt an honest man," added the last witness in triumph.

"But the point is, all four of you got a good look at the gem?" asked Birbal.

"Yes, yes," the witnesses replied.

"Fine," said Birbal. "Each witness will now retire to a separate room."

When they were gone, Birbal had a servant bring four lumps of soft wax.

"Take these to the witnesses and tell each to mold the wax into the shape of the diamond they saw Prakash holding."

Dhanlal shifted nervously from one foot to the other, as the entire court waited for the witnesses to reappear.

When they presented their lumps of wax, Birbal examined them, smiled, and handed them to the King.

One was the shape of a square, one was a hexagon, one a triangle, and the last was oblong. Clearly there had been no diamond, so each so-called witness had made the shape according to his own fancy.

Akbar looked up in anger.

"Let the false witnesses be given thirty lashes each. Let Dhanlal be given fifty lashes, and let Prakash be given the finest jewel that Dhanlal owns! And beware, swindler," said the King to Dhanlal. "The next time you cheat it will cost you your life!"

The jewelers and the witnesses were led away.

Akbar turned to Jai Mal and said:

"Worthy brother-in-law, you come from a family of great soldiers. I hereby give you the command of 10,000 knights. But Birbal shall be the Judge of Fatehpur Sikri."

Jai Mal was not satisfied, however, and to Akbar's great displeasure, he did not offer humble thanks but said:

"Your Majesty's wisdom is the finest pearl in the necklace of India's blessings. But I do not think this Birbal, who has only proved his mind runs along the same lines as farmers, quarreling housewives, and petty tricksters, should be exalted to the high rank of Judge. After all, a judge deals with matters of the state and the dignity of the Crown. Surely a judge should be a man of noble birth."

Behind the screen of marble the *Begam* swelled with pride at her brother's clever words. Akbar glared for a moment at his brother-in-law. Then he said:

"If you will abide by the results of one more test, I shall consider your point."

This time Jai Mal bowed with great humility.

"Hearing is obedience, *Jahanpanah*."

"Very well," said Akbar. "I shall submit another case to the two candidates at this hour, tomorrow morning."

And the courtiers all bowed as the Emperor strode from the Hall of Public Audience.

The Fourth Case:
The King's Mustache

AT BREAKFAST THE NEXT MORNING, Akbar still had not decided what test of wit he would give the two candidates. Suddenly his young son, Prince Sultan Salim, jumped up on his lap and playfully pulled his father's mustache. Not only did it hurt, but Akbar was sharply annoyed at having his thoughts disturbed.

"Get down!" shouted Akbar. "Why, do you know that anyone else, from the mountains of Kashmir to the shores of Bengal, could be put to death for pulling the Emperor's mustache?"

Prince Salim slunk down off the couch, crestfallen. But hardly had these words left his lips than Akbar smiled. Rising and wrapping his turban, he strode off to the Hall of Public Audience.

When Jai Mal and Birbal made their obeisance before the Throne, Akbar said:

"You have asked to try a case involving the dignity of the Crown. Very well. It will shock you to learn that this very morning somebody came into my presence and insulted your Emperor by actually pulling his mustache — "

The entire Court gasped.

Akbar held up his hand.

"Yes, I know. So I ask the distinguished candidates: what punishment fits this crime?"

Jai Mal stepped forward.

"Your Majesty, my father was a king, though he hardly approached the exalted excellence of your own glorious Presence. Nevertheless, the King's Person is sacred to the people. To insult the King is to insult our Motherland. Therefore, this rude person has committed treason against the state, and he should die."

Everyone nodded in agreement. Except Birbal.

"Does the other candidate agree?" asked the Emperor.

"*Maharaj*," said Birbal, smiling. "I would suggest that this 'culprit' be adorned with golden bracelets and receive sweets from the Emperor's own hand."

The courtiers and even the Queen behind her marble screen were puzzled. Jai Mal was aghast.

"Have you gone mad?" he gobbled at Birbal

But Akbar laughed out loud.

"Why do you recommend this sentence, Birbal?"

"Because, *Huzur*[5], I can hardly believe, in this well-guarded palace

5 "Presence," a title of respect given to Mughal nobles.

in the mightiest city on earth, that anyone could possibly have pulled the Imperial Mustache except your own little son, and Jai Mal's nephew, Prince Sultan Salim."

"Approach the Throne!" thundered the Great Mughal, rising. And turning to the assembled Court he said:

"Know that this man is appointed to the high rank of Judge of Fatehpur Sikri. His wise decisions shall be respected by all as the will of the Crown. And he shall be known from this day forward as Raja Birbal — Minister to the King!"

The Queen's Plot

THE QUEEN AND HER BROTHER Jai Mal were very bitter about Birbal's appointment as Judge. Jai Mal snarled:

"If Birbal had not been in my way, the appointment would have been mine for the taking."

"Your problem, brother," said the Queen, "is that you spend all your time hunting and trying on clothes. The Emperor has no faith in you."

"The Emperor loves hunting as much as I do," growled Jai Mal. "The problem is, this upstart has convinced Akbar that nobody can outsmart him. Now if only we could trap Birbal..."

"Ah," said the *Begam*, flashing a beautiful smile. "You and the Emperor may hunt tigers, but leave the art of trapping men to me..."

That evening when the Emperor entered his private apartments, the Queen began pouting, staring into the distance, and sighing repeatedly. At length Akbar looked up from a map of Gujarat that he had been studying and asked:

"How long are you going to be upset about your worthless brother not getting a job he doesn't deserve, Salima?"

The Queen's eyes snapped with fury.

"And who does deserve it — that son of village woodcutters? He has won over your mind, but Birbal is not half so clever as you think."

"Well," said the King, "even if I wanted to get rid of Birbal, I've already given him the appointment. I can hardly take it back for no reason."

"I can give you a reason."

"Really?" said Akbar. "What?"

"Give him some task to perform," said the Queen. "He is bound to fail. Then you can dismiss him for incompetence."

The King chuckled.

"Very well, Incomparable Pearl. You suggest the task."

Delighted, the Queen clutched Akbar's arm and whispered into his ear:

"When you are in the palace garden tomorrow, insist that Birbal bring me to you. He will not succeed, come what may."

Akbar agreed and laid her beautiful head upon his shoulder. The Queen smiled and thought:

"It is in my power now, Birbal, to see that you fail..."

Next morning, as birds murmured thoughtfully in the trees, Birbal chanced upon Akbar, looking very downcast in the rose garden.

"The cares of a King are written upon your brow, Great Presence."

"Birbal," answered Akbar, "it is the Empress. We have quarreled, and now she refuses to see me. But you could persuade her if anyone can. Go and bring her to me at once."

"Hearing is obedience, *Maharaj*."

"But if you fail," added Akbar, doing his best to smuggle a smile, "you will lose your position as Judge, and I will give it instead to the *Begam*'s brother, Jai Mal."

"I understand you, *Jahanpanah*," said Birbal, now also suppressing a smile.

He went without delay to the Queen's palace. At the gate, Birbal pulled a servant aside and commanded him:

"In five minutes come to me in the Queen's apartments. Give me this exact message — "

And Birbal told the servant what to say.

With his eyes respectfully on the floor, Birbal was ushered into the presence of the proud and lovely Queen.

"*Begam Sahiba*[6]," he began, "I bring you a message from His Majesty. He awaits you in the palace garden, and — "

But at that moment the obedient servant approached Birbal and tugged his sleeve.

"What is it?" asked Birbal, annoyed.

The servant shot a nervous look at the Queen.

"This is for your ears only, sir," mumbled the servant.

"Excuse me a moment, Your Highness," said Birbal, withdrawing politely — but not quite out of earshot — from the Queen.

---

[6] "My Lady Queen"

Curious as she was beautiful, the *Begam* crept up to the curtain that separated her from Birbal and heard the servant whisper these words:

"She — is — beautiful..."

The Queen stood up in shock. Birbal nodded, dismissed the servant, and returned to the Queen. He was grinning impudently as he told her:

"The situation has changed completely, *Begam Sahiba.* The King no longer needs you to come."

And Birbal slipped away, leaving the Empress afire with suspicion.

"Did I not hear the servant say something about a beautiful maiden?" she thought. "Is it possible the Emperor does not want me to see her with him?"

Unable to control her jealousy, the Queen ran from her palace and down the garden path. There she found Akbar alone, who looked up from smelling a rose.

"My dear wife!" he laughed. "You promised you would not come."

Stamping her foot, the Queen complained:

"I have been tricked into coming by your Minister, Birbal!"

"Tricked?" asked the King grinning. "If he told you a lie, I shall have him severely punished."

The *Begam* bit her lip.

"How can I tell him that fear of a beautiful rival brought me running?" she thought.

Out loud she said:

"No. All he told me was that the situation had changed."

Akbar roared laughing.

"That's all? You came because he only told you that?"

"I shall never forgive you," she snapped.

But Akbar put his strong arm around the Queen's slender shoulders, laid her head upon his chest, and said:

"You have too kind a heart not to forgive me, Incomparable Pearl. And one day you will also forgive Raja Birbal. Now, come, let us go to the reflecting pool and view the water lilies that have bloomed this morning... "

Birbal and the Pampered Queen

IT WAS NOT LONG before those words about forgiveness were proven true. One day Akbar took Birbal with him on a walk. Outside the Palace, they passed some women who had been pressed into hard labor. They were repairing the road, shoveling and breaking up solid rock. The Great Mughal was shocked at the difference between the hard life of these poor women and the luxury of his pampered Queen.

As soon as he got back to the palace, he gave an unheard-of order. From that day forward, the Queen would perform all the household tasks with her own hands.

"If women in the villages can work so hard when they are half starved," said Akbar, "there is no reason why women in my palace should lie about. It is ridiculous not to be able to dress yourself or comb your own hair. The Queen has been spoiled."

Now the Empress was a highborn noblewoman, used to milk baths and rare fragrances. She had always been surrounded by a dozen ladies-in-waiting. The sudden change from life in a cushioned harem to seamstress, cook, and washerwoman was too much for her delicate nature. Under the strain, she lost seven pounds in a week and never felt so wretched in her life. In desperation, she sent for Birbal.

When Birbal came to pay Her Majesty respects, he found her in an alarming state. But he tried to conceal his surprise.

"O Birbal," sobbed the Queen, "you are just the man I am looking for. Surely you can help me if anyone can. If I go on much longer like this, I am sure to die."

When Birbal heard the story of Akbar's strange command, he smiled, pondered, and then said:

"Give me five days, and I think I will make the King see the error of his ways."

"Five days!" cried the *Begam*. "You shall have my gratitude for five decades, if only you can move the King."

At the end of five days, Akbar decided to stroll through his garden of exotic plants. This park was a botanical library, growing the rarest and most beautiful plants in the world. They were tended by a highly talented gardener. So the Emperor was furious to find his prize plants all yellow and withered in the merciless Indian sun.

"Gardener!" he bellowed. "What have you done? What is the meaning of this neglect?"

"*Jahanpanah*," said the terrified gardener, "it is on Birbal's orders. I have not watered them for a week."

When Birbal was summoned before the Great Mughal, he was all sweetness and smiles.

"By Heaven, Birbal, what idiotic order have you given?"

"Idiotic, Majesty? But I was just reflecting. The great banyan trees grow strong and tall in the forest; yet we never water them. Why should these lazy garden plants have special treatment?"

"Fool!" thundered the King. "Anyone knows the most exotic plants are also the most frail."

But even as he spoke, Akbar remembered the harsh orders he had given for his delicate Queen.

Akbar and Birbal traded a sheepish smile.

And the ladies-in-waiting were again drawing the *Begam*'s bath of fragrant milk that afternoon.

Gallows of Gold

SO THE EMPRESS was reconciled to Raja Birbal. But her brother, Jai Mal, was certainly not. Jai Mal even sent a secret letter to King Abdullah of Uzbekistan, offering to help raise the banner of revolt against the Mughal Crown. But the letter was intercepted by spies and sent to Akbar. He was furious.

"This only proves," the King roared, "that nothing good can come from brothers-in-law. Let every brother-in-law in my Empire be hung!"

The court was shocked. Many noblemen protested, but the King would not listen.

"Carry out my orders," he fumed.

The courtiers were at a complete loss. Nobody wanted to be associated with an order that would earn the hatred of all the people. Then someone suggested:

"Let Birbal do it."

And, to everyone's surprise, Birbal agreed.

First, he went to Jai Mal.

"You may hate me, but know that the King read your letter to King Abdullah."

Jai Mal turned sickly white.

"This order against brothers-in-law is aimed at you," said Birbal.

"What can I do?" gasped Jai Mal.

"Will you give up plotting and promise lifelong loyalty to the King?"

"I will promise anything," stammered the terrified Prince.

"Well, let us see," said Birbal, and he went off to supervise the building of the gallows.

All over Fatehpur Sikri the dismal sound of hammering marked the final hour for thousands of innocent men. Gallows sprung up like weeds around the capital. On the fourth day, Birbal led the Emperor out on a balcony to view the forest of grisly gibbets.

"I thought you should see the preparations, *Jahanpanah*. Everything is almost ready."

The King surveyed the bristling execution ground with satisfaction. Then a brilliant flash in the morning sun caught his eye, and he peered carefully in its direction, shading his brow. Side by side stood two magnificently fashioned gallows, one of silver and another of gold.

"What sort of wasteful expenditure is that?" asked the King. "Who asked you to go and make gallows out of silver and gold?"

"It seemed only fitting," murmured Birbal somberly.

"Fitting?" asked Akbar, exasperated. "We are only hanging brothers-in-law here. For whom are these special gallows made?"

"The silver one," said Birbal, "is for my insignificant self, while the golden one, O Axis of the Earth, is for you."

"For me?" exclaimed the Emperor. "Who dares to send me to the gallows?"

"You go upon your own orders, *Maharaj*. For if Jai Mal is brother-in-law to you, you also are a brother-in-law to Jai Mal. Tomorrow, as the most distinguished of brothers-in-law, you must hang first, to be followed by this brother-in-law, and just about everybody else."

The Emperor kicked a pebble with his foot.

"Oh, very well," he grumbled. "Call the whole thing off."

And all the gallows in the land were put to the flame.

Jai Mal kept his pledge of loyalty to Akbar — but he had promised Birbal nothing, and he continued to plot against him.

Duck Soup

WHEN BIRBAL HAD secured his fortune at court, the first person he thought of was his mother. He returned to his native village, Tikawanpur, on the banks of the river Jumna, and brought her back to Fatehpur Sikri in a splendid caravan. He gave her a luxurious wing of his shimmering palace and provided every comfort and pleasure his mother could desire.

Birbal's mother was wonderfully proud of her clever and generous son. As soon as she got over the surprise of so many incredible dreams come true, she began sending a stream of joyful letters to her relatives back in the village. The people of Tikawanpur could hardly believe her stories of life in the elegant court of Shah Akbar.

Before long, some of Birbal's poor relations began to ask themselves,

"Why should we not share some of the glory that our cousin

Birbal has earned?"

So, one of Birbal's cousins decided to make the journey to the fabled city of Fatehpur Sikri to seek out Birbal's fortune.

"I should not go empty-handed," thought the cousin. He chose the fattest duckling from the animals on his farm and went his way.

When he entered the gates of Fatehpur Sikri, he was just as astonished as Birbal had been when he had made his first journey there as Mahesh Das. The country cousin was even more amazed at Birbal's fame — everyone in the bazaar knew how to direct him to Birbal's house. And what a house! It was a palace of towering red sandstone with courtly gardens and laughing fountains. No one in Tikawanpur had ever dreamed of such a home.

Timidly, the cousin made his way through fretted columns to the *diwan*[7]. A servant on whispering feet went to announce his arrival to Birbal. In mere moments, Birbal appeared, dressed in gorgeous garments of silk and gold.

"Welcome! Welcome!" he laughed. "Since you are from my village of Tikawanpur, you are my brother. But please, friend, let me know your name."

"I...I am your cousin," stammered the villager. "And I have brought you this...this duck."

"Splendid!" cried Birbal. "Then we shall have him roasted for lunch."

Birbal clapped his hands, and servants appeared as if from nowhere. They took the duck to the kitchen and the country cousin to a magnificent chamber, where he took a hot bath and dressed in new and

---

[7] Salon.

costly robes. When he had rested, the servants brought him to the banquet hall. There he sat down with Birbal to a feast of a hundred exquisite dishes. In the center of the table was a crisp, magnificent, roast duck.

"Now tell me the news of Tikawanpur," smiled Birbal. And the cousins enjoyed a happy afternoon together.

The next day, Birbal loaded his cousin with princely gifts and sent him on his way.

Back in Tikawanpur, the villagers were dazzled with his tales of Birbal's wealth and position of honor.

"Everyone in the capital speaks of him as if he were the Emperor himself," declared the cousin. "They say he is the Emperor's best friend, and the splendor of his surroundings proves it!"

"Then everything his mother wrote was true!" cried the villagers. And all of Birbal's other cousins decided to make a journey to the city to claim their share of Birbal's wealth.

The next week, another of Birbal's distant relatives walked the long road to Fatehpur Sikri. While he was waiting to be announced at Birbal's house, he suddenly remembered that he had forgotten to bring a gift. When Birbal appeared, thinking quickly, he stammered,

"I am a cousin of the cousin who brought you the duck."

Smiling, Birbal said, "Welcome, brother." And he dressed the villager in gorgeous robes, treated him to a banquet of a hundred dishes, and sent him home laden with precious gifts.

The next week, another villager from Tikawanpur appeared at Birbal's house and said,

"I am a cousin of the cousin of the cousin who brought you the duck."

Smiling, Birbal again gave the man rich garments to wear, presented a sumptuous feast, and sent him home with costly gifts.

The next week, another villager from Tikawanpur arrived and said,

"I am a cousin of the cousin of the cousin of the cousin who brought you the duck."

This time Birbal smiled a little less, but he invited the man in, gave him luxurious robes, feasted him, and sent him home with gifts.

The next week, another villager from Tikawanpur arrived and told Birbal,

"I am a cousin of the cousin of the cousin of the cousin of the cousin who brought you the duck."

At last Birbal was tired of feasting his lazy cousins from Tikawanpur who all wanted something for nothing. So he invited the villager in, gave him beautiful robes to wear, and then went to the kitchen and told his chef, "Boil some water."

When the water was hot, he said,

"Pour the hot water into two soup bowls and bring them for our lunch."

Birbal sat down with his country cousin, smiled, and, when the hot water was placed before them, he said, with a magnificent gesture,

"Eat in good health!"

The villager stared blankly at the water in the saucer. Then he sipped it. He tasted nothing.

"What is this?" he asked.

"Ah," grinned Birbal, "that is the soup of the soup of the soup of the soup of the soup of the duck that your cousin brought."

And after spooning all the water down with great relish, Birbal sent his cousin back to the village empty-handed.

From that day forward, Birbal had no more unwanted visitors from Tikawanpur.

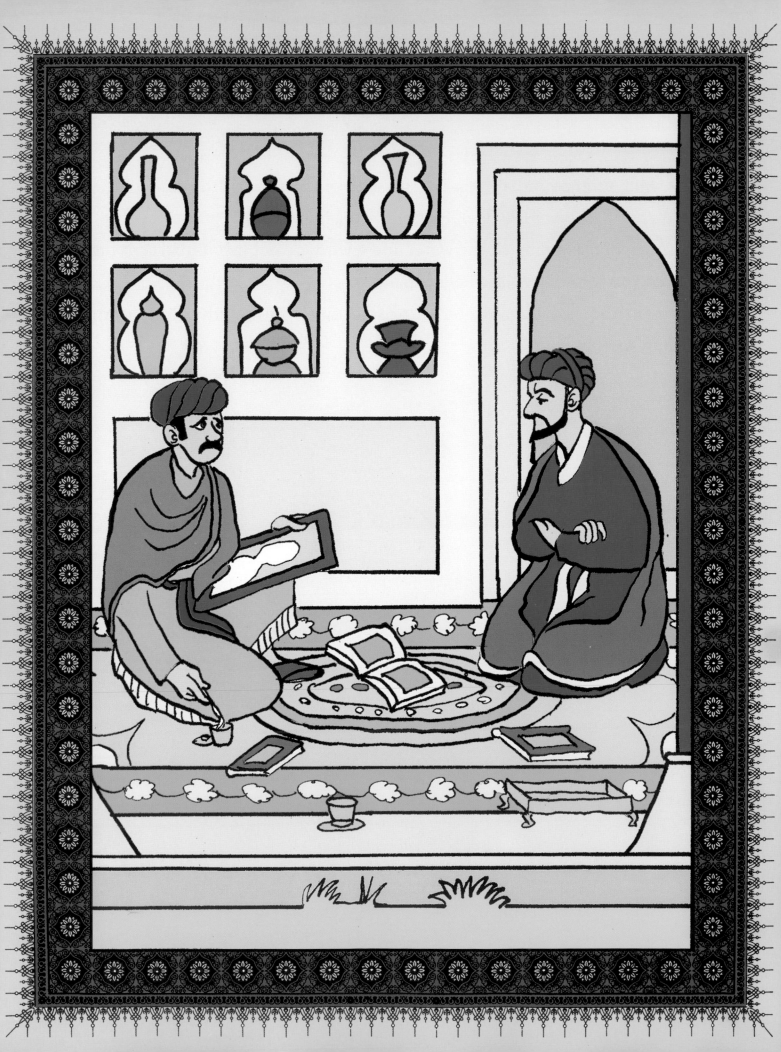

The Patron of the Arts

WHEN AKBAR BECAME KING, he personally visited his royal studio of painters every week, judging new masterpieces and rewarding the most talented artists.

Akbar especially liked the works of a humble painter named Daswant. Although Daswant came from a poor family, he became the First Master of the Age, another Jewel in the Mughal Crown.

Many of the courtiers imitated the Emperor, commissioning paintings from his artists. But one nobleman, Munim Khan, had no wish to waste money on scribbling fools.

One day in *Durbar*[8], the Emperor said, "Munim Khan has proven a loyal subject. But I do not think a nobleman is truly noble if he shows no interest in the arts."

Taking the hint, Munim Khan sent for Daswant, who dutifully came to the Khan's beautiful home.

"I don't see the point in it, but just to please the Emperor, I want

[8] Imperial Court or Hall of Public Audience.

to commission a painting from you. They say you have talent."

Daswant bowed low and humbly murmured, "Your praise is too kind, *Huzur*."

"Probably it is," frowned Munim Khan. "But let's see how good you are. What will it cost to have you paint my portrait?"

"The usual fee is 100 silver rupees, sir," said Daswant.

Munim Khan choked. "A hundred silver rupees! That's robbery!"

"That is the usual fee," said Daswant firmly.

"Very well," scowled the Khan. "You shall have your fee, but I warn you, the painting must be an exact likeness of me. If not, you shall not get even a copper *paisa*[9]."

"Hearing is obedience, O Munificent One," smiled Daswant. And he went to work, making studies and sketches of Munim Khan's head. At the end of the day, he went back to his studio to finish the portrait.

After a week's hard work, Daswant returned to the home of Munim Khan, proudly bearing a beautiful portrait, trimmed in paint of silver and gold.

But Munim Khan scowled and said, "This doesn't look anything like me. Look here, you have painted me with a beard."

Daswant was astonished. He looked and, indeed, Munim Khan had shaved off his beard! Only his long mustache was left.

"But, sir, you had a beard when I painted you," said Daswant.

"I said a perfect likeness, and this does not look like me. Do it right, or you shall not be paid."

So Daswant took out his pencils and paper and made new sketches of

[9] Penny.

Munim Khan wearing only his mustache. Then he went back to his studio, and, after a week of tireless work, brought back a lovely new portrait in ruby and sapphire hues.

But Daswant halted in his tracks when he saw the Khan — now he had shaved off his mustache, too!

Munim Khan picked up the portrait, shook his head, and said, "No. As you can see, it looks nothing like me. This fellow has a mustache. I do not. Try again."

Sadly, Daswant made sketches of the clean-shaven Munim Khan, went back to work, and returned in one week with a new masterpiece.

"What will it be now?" Daswant wondered. He soon found out. The Khan reappeared with his beard and mustache growing back.

"This is not an exact likeness," said Munim Khan, frowning at the clean-shaven portrait. "If you can show me an exact likeness of myself, you shall have a hundred silver rupees. If not, you shall have nothing. And to think," he sneered, "they call you 'First Master of the Age'..."

A miserable Daswant headed homeward through the streets of Fatehpur Sikri. On the way, he ran into Birbal.

"Why so down?" smiled Birbal. "Have you run out of subjects to paint?"

"Run out!" cried Daswant. "I just wish I could pin one down!" And he explained his problem.

Birbal laughed.

"Come to *Durbar* tomorrow," he told Daswant. "With the Emperor's help, we will set everything right."

Munim Khan was in the Hall of Public Audience early the next day. When Akbar had finished the serious business of state, he asked if any of his ministers had further matters.

Birbal stepped forward.

"Sire," he said, "I have heard that Munim Khan offers 100 silver rupees to the artist who will show him an exact likeness of himself."

Akbar was pleased. "Is this true?" he asked the Khan.

"Yes, Your Majesty," murmured Munim Khan, looking darkly at Birbal.

"I also have heard that Daswant himself has failed three times to pass the test," Birbal said

Akbar was astonished. "My most talented artist?" he cried.

Daswant bowed his head. "Yes, Sire, it is true. Munim Khan is a very difficult subject to paint."

"Well, Sire," said Birbal, "I would like to earn the 100 silver rupees myself."

"You, Birbal?" grinned Akbar. "You can't even draw a straight line! How can you succeed where Daswant has failed?"

"Does Munim Khan agree that he will pay 100 silver rupees to any artist who can show him an exact likeness of himself?"

"By the beard of the Prophet," swore Munim Khan.

"Well, then, here you are." And Birbal handed Munim Khan a mirror.

Munim Khan grew red-faced. "How dare you play such games with me?" he shouted. "This is no portrait, it's, it's — "

"It's an exact likeness of yourself." smiled Birbal.

"You swore by the beard of the Prophet!" laughed the Emperor.

"Bah," growled Munim Khan. "You are an artist, indeed, Birbal!" And he threw Birbal the hundred silver coins.

"And you, Munim Khan Sahib" replied Birbal, tossing the bag of coins to Daswant, "are at last a patron of the arts!"

Fate

ONE DAY AKBAR AND BIRBAL rode out hunting with a huge and colorful entourage. After several hot hours of hard riding, the two got separated from the other sportsmen in a dense jungle. Akbar was furious.

"Look, I'm King," he grumbled to Birbal. "How is it possible to be surrounded by courtiers stupid enough to actually lose me?"

But Birbal was calm.

"Everything is a matter of Fate, Your Majesty. Good may come of it," he said.

Akbar was annoyed, but he said nothing as they rode in search of water. Finally he burst out:

"My Empire contains a thousand mighty rivers, yet I can't even find a puddle to slake my thirst!"

"It may work out for the best," remarked Birbal.

These words had hardly left his lips when the two broke into a clearing with a small well. Akbar reined in his horse.

"At last! Birbal, dismount and fetch me a drink."

"Hearing is obedience, Sire." And, so saying, Birbal slipped from his saddle and headed for the well.

As Akbar began to dismount, however, his finger snagged one of the glistening arrows in his quiver, and the King cried out in pain.

"Now look what's happened!" he shouted, trying to stop the flow of blood. "My fat doctor is probably gobbling a hot lunch in camp while I bleed! Could anything else possibly go wrong?"

"Everything happens for the best," murmured Birbal, raising water from the well.

But Akbar had heard this one time too many.

"How dare you say such stupid, shallow things when I'm in pain?" bellowed the King. And, in a fit of anger, he flung Birbal down the well.

The gratifying splash made Akbar feel immediately better. But he had hardly started to peer over the edge of the well when he felt the unmistakable prickling of eyes upon his back.

Wheeling around, he discovered to his horror that he was surrounded by half-naked tribals, all of whom had their poisoned arrows trained upon his heart. Getting a grip on himself, he drew up to his full height and announced:

"I am Shah Akbar of Hindustan. Kneel before your Emperor!"

But the tribals only rattled their bows threateningly. One of them stepped forward, croaking:

"Whoever you may be, I am Todar, chief of the cannibals in these parts. We are going to sacrifice you to the Death Goddess, Durgha!"

"Help, Birbal!" wailed the King. But the black depths of the well returned no sound.

The cannibals dragged the helpless Mughal and bound him to the altar of their goddess. But just as everything was ready for the sacrifice, one of the tribals noticed the blood still dripping from Akbar's finger.

"Stop!" he cried out. The cannibal chief saw the bleeding finger, and he spat angrily on the grass.

"What bad luck," said Todar. "Everyone knows you cannot offer a sacrifice to the goddess if it is imperfect. That cut finger has saved this fellow's life. Too bad. He looks like he would have been a tasty one."

Intensely relieved and rewinding his trampled turban, the Great Mughal limped back to the clearing and bashfully hallooed for Birbal down the well. This time there was an answer.

"I'm so sorry," said the King, as he guiltily hauled Birbal up. "You were quite right. Everything does happen for the best."

"Yes, *Maharaj*," said Birbal.

But as Birbal was wringing the water from his clothes, the King suddenly had a thought.

"Just tell me this," said Akbar mischievously to his sodden friend. "Though my cut finger did save me, what benefit did you get from being thrown down a well?"

Birbal grinned.

"Since my finger was not cut, going down a well was the only thing that saved me from being sacrificed in your place! That every adversity contains the seed of a greater benefit, *Jahanpanah*, is what I call — Fate."

The Donkey's Haircut

THE COURT BARBER was an arrogant fellow. He had served both Akbar's father and his grandfather. He considered himself almost part of the dynasty. As such, he also trimmed the beards of some of the wealthiest and most cultured men in Fatehpur Sikri. This lofty company made the barber feel greedy and somewhat above the law.

One day, a poor old woodcutter trudged into the city market after a long morning in the mountains splitting logs and tying them into bundles. His broken-down old donkey — a companion of fifteen years — swayed under his burden of firewood.

As the woodcutter plodded past the barber's shop, calling his wares, the barber poked his head through the curtains and yelled:

"How much for everything on that donkey?"

"Five copper *paisa*, sir," said the woodcutter.

"I'll give you four," sniffed the barber, counting the coins down on the bench before him.

The old woodcutter shrugged and said:

"Mine is a fair price, but these are hard times."

So he off-loaded his bundles, took the money, and led his donkey on the homeward path.

But he had hardly gone half a mile when he remembered that his ax had been tied up in the bundles of firewood, and he would need it for the next morning's work.

Running back to the barbershop, he panted:

"*Huzur*, I would not have bothered you, but those bundles I sold you — my ax is tied up in one of them, and I shall need it for tomorrow. I go to the hills to chop firewood two hours before dawn... "

But the barber was busy with a wealthy caravan merchant and growled:

"Go away."

"But, sir, my ax — it is more precious than diamonds to me, sir. I cannot support my family without it, and I certainly cannot afford to buy another — "

"I told you to be gone!" shouted the barber. "You sold me everything on your donkey for four copper *paisa*, and if your ax was bound up with that load, so much the worse for you. Now go, before I call the city guards!"

Miserable, the woodcutter staggered away. He was faced with complete ruin, and he did not know what to do. Then, for some reason, he thought of the new Judge, Birbal, whom all the people had been gossiping about. He asked a spice merchant for directions and headed immediately to Birbal's house.

"We can take the matter before the King," said Birbal, "but I think, in the case of this rich and influential barber, he will win. After all, you admit you did agree to sell him everything on your donkey... "

"But what can I do?" wailed the woodcutter. "Without the ax, my family will starve!"

"Listen to me," said Birbal sharply, and the woodcutter closed his mouth. "Here is what you will do... "

And on Birbal's instructions, the woodcutter went the next morning to the barber's stall and said:

"Friend barber, I apologize for making that scene yesterday. After thinking about it, I realized you were right. Will you please let bygones be bygones?"

"Hmf," said the barber. "Why not?"

"Oh, thank you," smiled the woodcutter. "Then will you also let me know what you would charge to shave myself and a companion?"

The barber looked at the woodcutter with dislike. He was not used to such shabby customers. But the barber had a policy — never say no, just name a higher price.

"Twenty silver rupees," he snapped. To his amazement, the woodcutter agreed, immediately counting the coins down on the barber's bench.

Shrugging, the barber put them in his moneybox and shaved the woodcutter. When he had finished, he asked:

"Now where's your companion?"

"There," said the woodcutter, pointing to his donkey.

"A donkey!" shouted the barber. "Why you stupid, impudent oaf! Get out of here and never show your face at my shop again!"

But at that moment Birbal wandered by and heard the explanations of both men.

"This is a difficult case," said the Judge. "I would like to put it to the King."

There were many curious spectators when the barber and the woodcutter brought their complaints before the Throne.

When Akbar had heard the matter of the ax, he turned to the woodcutter sadly and said:

"I am sorry for you, my son, but a deal is a deal. If the barber were generous, he would not hesitate to return your ax. But I am afraid I cannot force him to do this."

But when the case went on, and Akbar heard the story of the donkey, he burst out laughing:

"I suspect you have had a very good advisor, woodcutter, and all I can say is: a deal is a deal! Barber, you will have to honor your side."

So the miserable barber was forced to soap down the donkey and shave him bald as a pomegranate, ruining seven good razors. All the while, dozens of chuckling noblemen and shopkeepers looked on.

"A little more off the top!" called one.

"Don't nick him, or we'll demand a refund!" cried another.

"Don't stint on the perfume!" shouted a third. And the crowd rippled with laughter.

No sooner had the woodcutter begun to lead his fragrant and chilly donkey away than another wag led a camel to the barbershop and shouted:

"How much to shave a little off the hump?"

Surrounded by giggles and jeers from the entire bazaar, the barber grabbed the woodcutter's ax and ran, red-faced, after him.

"Here!" he screamed, thrusting it into the old man's hands. "Take your cursed ax and never darken my doorstep again! And the rest of you buffoons," he called to the crowd, "why don't you find something useful to do?"

The barber stormed back to his shop and snapped its curtains shut behind him.

From that day forward, he nursed a bitter grudge against Raja Birbal.

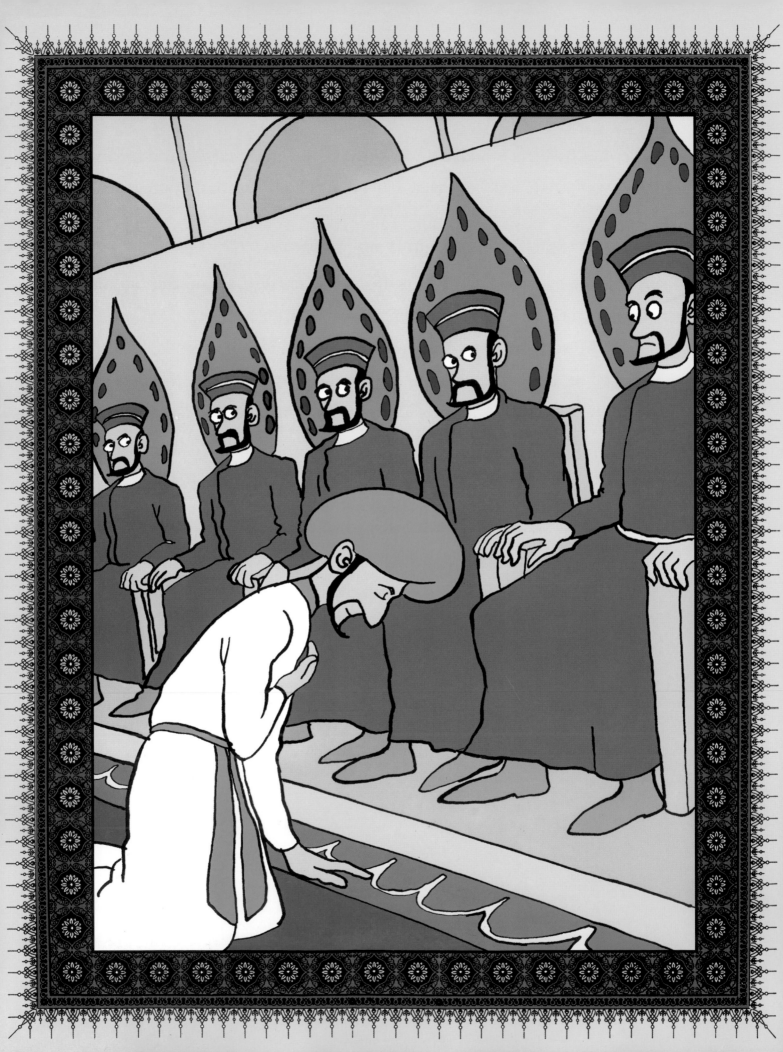

Birbal and the Persian Shah

BEFORE AKBAR WAS BORN, his father, the Emperor Humayun, had lost his throne. He, his Queen, and a few loyal friends fled to Persia to escape their enemies and accept the protection of that munificent monarch, Shah Tahmasp.

Before they reached the territory of Persia, Akbar was born at Amerkot, on October 15, 1542. When Humayun saw his newborn son, he handed a piece of fragrant musk to each in his small circle of friends and said:

"May the fame of my son fill the world, as this musk perfumes the air. I shall call him Akbar, which means Most Great."

Akbar did, of course, become a very great king, but Shah Abbas of Persia never let him forget the favors his father had done Humayun and the Mughal family. He always addressed the

Mughal Emperor as "Younger Brother" in his letters and found a hundred other ways to imply that Akbar's glittering fame was all because of the generous Persian Shah.

"It is said," Akbar commented one day, "that whoever receives a favor should never forget it. But whoever does a favor should never mention it. I wonder if this proverb is current in Persia... "

Still, Akbar let the matter go. Then one day, the Shah began to think of waging war on India and adding Akbar's Empire to his own. Yet travelers told so many marvels of the Mughal Court, Shah Abbas thought it would be wise to know more about India before trying to invade it. The Shah asked Akbar to send him an ambassador, who could inform him of the wonders of Hindustan.

Akbar wanted to impress the Shah once and for all, so he selected Birbal as his emissary, loading him down with the treasures of India as gifts for the Persian King.

When Birbal reached Ispahan, he was conducted with music and pomp into the Presence Chamber, as befitted an envoy of the Great Mughal. But Birbal's gaze fell upon a most astonishing sight: instead of one throne, there were five — and upon them, five identical Shahs!

"It is a test," thought Birbal. "Yet I must quickly decide which is the true Shah and bow to him, or he will take offense."

Letting his eyes travel down the row of thrones, Birbal suddenly smiled, knelt respectfully before one of the shahs, and said:

"My lord and master, Akbar, Emperor of India, conveys his felicitations and respects to the exalted Shahinshah of Persia."

"Raja Birbal," laughed the Shahinshah. "You have never seen us before. How did you recognize us?"

"Your Majesty," said Birbal. "As I stood perplexed, I noticed that all the other 'shahs' looked at you for your reaction, while you alone fixed your gaze on me."

Marveling at Birbal's keen sense of observation, the Shah replied:

"Truly you are an ocean of intelligence, Raja Birbal. But tell me, now that you have traversed many kingdoms on your journey here, what can you say about me in comparison with other kings?"

"Your Majesty is the Full Moon, while the other kings are only glowworms."

The King of Persia smiled.

"And how do I compare with my younger brother, Akbar of Hindustan?" he asked.

Birbal answered promptly:

"The Emperor Akbar is the New Moon."

The Shah was delighted and loaded Birbal with gifts for his return home.

But news of Birbal's beautiful compliment to the Persian King reached India before him, and Akbar was very angry. He brushed the gifts from Ispahan aside and thundered:

"Birbal, you have betrayed and insulted me! How dare you call the Persian Shah the Full Moon, while comparing me to nothing but a crescent?"

"*Jahanpanah*," replied Birbal, "the Full Moon grows smaller day by day, while the New Moon has all its glory before it."

Akbar laughed and embraced his friend, while the spies in Fatehpur Sikri swiftly conveyed this conversation back to the Shah.

"The wisdom of Akbar's advisors," said Shah Abbas, "makes our sages seem like fools."

And never again did he contemplate war against the mighty ruler of Hindustan.

Cats

ONE DAY IN THE KING'S COUNCIL, Akbar proposed a war against Burma. He asked his nobles: "What do you think?"

"Burma must be crushed!" snarled one.

"The Iravati River shall run red with blood," growled another.

"May your shadow darken the frontiers of China," thundered a third.

"But wouldn't a war so far in the East invite a revolt in Gujarat or Kabul?" asked Akbar. "And is Burma a rich enough prize to justify that risk?"

"Not in the least," said one nobleman.

"Quite a waste of our forces," said another.

"Your glory would grow by refusing to conquer so unworthy an enemy," blustered a third.

On the way home from the Council Chamber, Akbar was depressed.

"My courtiers obey me blindly, whatever I order them to do," he thought, "Since none of them dares to contradict the King, how can I know whether my plans are wise or foolish? I need to find out which of the nobles has the wisdom to correct me if my plans are bad, but the tact not to disobey my orders."

So the next morning, as the court assembled in the marble Hall of Public Audience, the King addressed his nobles, saying:

"I have decided that cats are the finest animals in the world. Do you agree?"

"By all means, *Jahanpanah*," murmured some.

"So say the sages of old," observed others.

"I have often thought of this, but lacked the wisdom to express it," chimed the rest.

"Very well," grinned Akbar. "I order each of you to keep a hundred cats. At the end of every month, you shall parade them at court — and I want to see that each man's cats are healthy, sleek, and fat!"

The noblemen bowed respectfully. But inwardly they cursed their flattering tongues.

"You had to go and agree with the King!" accused some.

"And you had to agree with those who agreed with the King!" said others.

"And you had to agree with those who agreed with those who agreed with the King!" wailed the rest.

Rich as all of them were, the noblemen calculated how much milk for a hundred cats would cost — astronomical!

Nevertheless, the Imperial edict went forth, and every courtier scrambled to furnish himself with a hundred cats. It was astonishing how the price of sleek, fat felines rose in the bazaar. A day before, kittens were given away or drowned — now the mangiest stray cost more than rubies.

Every month, the courtiers paraded their precious, pampered cats before the King, who rewarded or punished them according to the seeming contentment of their pets. The nobles fretted night and day that one of their cats would lose its appetite or run away and that they would have less than a full hundred to bring to the Palace at the end of the month. And, of course, it was not long before a hundred cats became a thousand, and the courtiers were nearly driven from their homes.

"You ignore your children if they catch fever or go in ragged clothes," their wives shouted, "but if a cat skips a meal, you lose a night of sleep!"

"You just don't understand the King," they whimpered to their wives.

And the affairs of the Kingdom suffered, for the courtiers were too exhausted to fulfill their duties in the King's Council. Still the Emperor said nothing.

At length Birbal, who was allergic to cats in the first place, decided that enough was enough. Summoning his cook, he said:

"Tonight you will boil the cats' milk. Serve it to them only when it is hot enough to scald brass."

The cook did as he was ordered. When Birbal's multitude of cats approached their golden saucers, a hiss rent the air as their tongues burnt and their whiskers singed from the unexpectedly hot milk. Yowling and spitting, the cats scrambled into the shrubs and trees, and they drank not a drop of the scorching milk.

For the rest of the month Birbal kept this up, until every one of his starving cats ran from the mere sight of milk and became a sorry bag of bones.

On the day of the Emperor's cat parade, the other courtiers gawked at Birbal's scrawny cats, saying:

"Now, surely, Birbal is doomed."

Akbar reviewed every cat with his usual care, rewarding and punishing the nobles, according to the happiness of their cats. But when Birbal produced his cats, the Emperor flew into a rage.

"How dare you flaunt my Royal Command? I want to see fat and healthy cats! Your animals are no more than sacks of skin! You shall be exiled for this, Birbal — or worse!"

But with respectfully downcast eyes, Birbal replied:

"O God's Shadow Upon the Earth, the problem is not with me, but with these cats. They have developed a hatred of milk. None of them will even go near it."

"Not like milk?" thundered the King. "Who ever heard of such a cat? Ridiculous."

His fingers crisped to a nearby servant. "Bring a saucer of milk at once!"

But when a plate of milk was set before Birbal's cats, the mere sight of it reminded them of scorched tongues and wilted whiskers, and they ran spitting and yowling behind curtains, beneath cushions, and even under the Peacock Throne. Then the plump cats of the other nobles waddled over to the plate of milk and licked it dry.

"Truly," said the King in wonder. "These are cats of a different color. Birbal, how do you explain it?"

Birbal smiled.

"How do you explain anything, *Jahanpanah*? Strange are the whims of cats and kings."

Unable to contain his laughter, Akbar rose, wiping the tears from his eyes, and said:

"Birbal, you have made an excellent point. You have shown, with respect and wisdom, that this was a bad idea from the start. From now on, you shall be the Chief Advisor in the King's Council. And as for the rest of you — none of you need any longer keep a cat."

So, all the cats were driven with a vengeance from the city. And that evening there was great rejoicing — among all of Fatehpur Sikri's mice.

Birbal and the Seller of Oil

IN THE GREAT BAZAAR there was an oil merchant, who was known for the fine quality and freshness of his mustard oil from Kashmir. He was always very busy.

One morning, he had sold almost all his oil and was just sitting down for a moment's rest. A flour merchant, who had been carefully eyeing all the coins the oil seller had been stuffing into his money pouch, wandered over to his stall and said:

"Give me some oil."

Rising, the oilman reached for his jar of oil, drained a full measure into a clay pot, sealed it, and handed it over the counter.

But, rather than take money from his own purse, the flour merchant snatched the oilman's pouch from the counter where it was resting.

"What are you doing?" cried the oilman.

"Fool! Can't you see I am taking money from my purse to pay you for the oil?"

"Your purse? That purse is mine!"

"Nonsense," sniffed the flour merchant. "This money pouch was given to me years ago by my wife. You are either a thief or mad. Keep your oil. I want nothing to do with you."

And he turned on his heel. But in a single bound the oilman leaped over his counter and seized the flour merchant by his sleeve. As they scuffled, other merchants in the bazaar ran forward and dragged them apart.

"Thief!" shrieked one.

"Cheat!" howled the other.

"Quiet!" boomed a blacksmith. "We need a judge. Let us take the matter to the King."

"The King!" sneered the flour merchant. "Do you think the King has time to get mixed up in the quarrels of petty crooks like this man here?" He jabbed a derisive finger at the oilman.

"Silence!" thundered the blacksmith. "You are right. But if this is too small a matter for the King, we can go to the house of Birbal. He can solve any problem."

The flour merchant wanted to object, but all the merchants shouted, "Yes! Yes!" And the two enemies were marched off in front of a cheering crowd.

Birbal invited the merchants to sit with him upon a silken rug, as courteously as if they had been nobles. He listened to the episode without interrupting. Then he glanced from one man to the other.

"Give me the purse," he commanded.

The blacksmith wrested it from the clutches of the flour merchant and offered it respectfully to Birbal.

Casually, Birbal opened the pouch, and, as he was counting the coins inside, he said: "You must be the most popular oil seller in Fatehpur Sikri."

"I...I..." The oilman was tongue-tied in the unexpected elegance of his surroundings.

"He is," confirmed the blacksmith.

"I suppose you are extremely busy, pouring, measuring, and capping your oil?" Birbal went on.

"O Brightest Eminence," said the oilman. "From dawn to noon I have no time even to pause for a sip of rosewater."

The flour merchant smiled to himself. "This Birbal is a talkative half-wit," he thought. "He is buying time because he knows the oilman cannot prove that the money pouch is not mine."

But, even as he had these thoughts, the flour-monger felt the cold stare of Birbal upon him.

"Bring me," said Birbal to his servants, "a pot filled with boiling water."

Everyone exchanged puzzled glances, but when the pot was set before him, Birbal dropped the money pouch into the boiling water. Burning with curiosity, the flour merchant, the oilman, the blacksmith, and all the merchants peered into the pot as well. Before their eyes, beads of oil rose to the surface of the water, forming a sheen of rainbow-colored rings. Then Birbal pointed at the steaming surface.

"Oil," he commented. "A money bag so drenched with oil could only belong to an oil merchant."

Staggering back, the flour merchant fell to his knees.

"Please, *Huzur*, it was only a misunderstanding..."

"Silence!" Birbal scolded. "You will pay the oilman seven gold *mohurs*[10] and spend forty days in jail."

There was a murmur of admiration from the assembled merchants. The flour monger hung his head, and Raja Birbal's fame increased.

---

[10] Coin of the Mughal Imperial Mint.

Currying Favor

AKBAR LOVED TO TEST Birbal's keen mind. Many jealous courtiers tried to compete with Birbal for the King's friendship, but they were in an unequal battle of wits.

One day in *Durbar*, the Emperor asked Birbal:

"You were at a wedding yesterday, were you not? Tell me, Birbal, what was there to eat?"

"Let's see," mused Birbal. "There was festive rice, lentils, chicken kebabs..."

"What else?" asked Akbar.

"Seer fish, yogurt and cucumbers, lamb..."

"What else?" asked Akbar.

"Spinach and homemade cheese, chick peas, rotis[11], almond sweets..."

At that moment, a messenger arrived from the Deccan[12] with

[11] Flatbread.
[12] South India.

important news for the King. The conversation with Birbal was interrupted, as Akbar went into council with his generals.

A week later in *Durbar*, Akbar decided to test Birbal's memory. He turned to him without warning and said, "What else, Birbal?"

"Curry," answered Birbal promptly.

Akbar was delighted.

"Magnificent!" laughed the King. "Curry, indeed! Here, Birbal, take this emerald as a reward!"

The other courtiers, who had completely forgotten the conversation of a week ago, were baffled at what they had seen. When *Durbar* was over, they met in the garden.

"Did you see the size of the emerald the Emperor gave Birbal?" asked one.

"And all Birbal said was 'curry!'" said another.

"The Emperor must truly love curry," said a third. "If he gave Birbal an emerald just for saying curry, what would he give for the real thing?"

"Let's give the Emperor what he wants. Then we shall all earn a fabulous reward!"

The courtiers rubbed their hands in glee.

Next day they arrived at the Hall of Public Audience carrying huge cauldrons on their heads.

"What in the world are you doing?" demanded Akbar.

"May we be your sacrifice, O Wisdom of the Age," said a courtier, laying his cauldron at the Emperor's feet. "We have brought you some of the delicious curry you so greatly admire." And the others fawningly set their pots of curry before the Throne.

Akbar realized at once what was happening. He and Birbal rolled their eyes. Then the King blurted:

"You fools! Birbal was rewarded for his memory. Now you shall carry the reward of your stupidity away in your stomachs. Each of you shall eat all the useless curry you have brought!"

And the Emperor and Birbal watched the miserable noblemen eat curry, and eat curry, and eat curry, until their stomachs almost burst.

Greater Than God?

AKBAR GREW VERY FOND of Birbal, and, although he was a busy king, doing more in a single day than most people do in a week, he found time to chat with his new companion and learn from his ready wit. He gave Birbal money and land, so that he could live comfortably as a minister to the Crown. This aroused the envy of the many courtiers who fluttered around Akbar.

One evening, Akbar invited Birbal, and many other courtiers, to a feast. A hundred exquisite dishes were the minimum ever served for the King's repast. Yet, as Akbar looked over the ocean of food placed before him in such beautiful array, he became sad and called for his cook.

"Is it right," he asked, "for a king to have so much and only one stomach? Among my subjects there may be many empty stomachs and nothing to go in them tonight. Take some of this food into the street and let the poor eat first. When they have been satisfied, come back and tell us, and then we will begin."

Many of the nobles were annoyed at having their dinner delayed. But Akbar called for a storyteller to keep the courtiers amused. Akbar loved stories.

The old storyteller spun many wonderful tales of long ago. Akbar rewarded him with a bag of gold. So surprised was he at the generosity of this gift, the storyteller blurted out: "Truly, *Maharaj*, you are the greatest king who ever lived. O Axis of the Earth, you are greater even than God..."

Immediately, a mulla, a religious man, sprung to his feet and thundered:

"That is blasphemy, *Jahanpanah!* No one can be greater than God! I demand that the storyteller be punished to the full extent of the law."

Akbar realized that the old man simply had been overexcited by the splendor of the King's reward.

"Perhaps," thought the King, "I should have given him a little less."

Of course, God would not be affected by the old man's foolish remark. But the law against using God's name in vain was the law...

While Akbar was thinking these things, the storyteller grew faint with terror. The mulla shuddered in righteous indignation. Then Akbar happened to glance at Birbal, who, as usual in tense moments, wore an unfathomable half-smile.

"Your Majesty," murmured Birbal. "I do not think this is a case of blasphemy. I agree with the old man. In a way you are greater than God."

Now Akbar was really shocked. The old man had spoken foolishly. But this was Birbal! The mulla stammered angrily, unable to form words.

"How many of you," asked Akbar, turning to the rest of the assembled courtiers, "would say that your Emperor is greater than God?"

The courtiers, who had been enjoying the storyteller's discomfort, were now struck dumb. Not one of them was ready to offend God... but neither did any of them want to insult the King. They looked at Birbal's serene smile and then at the red-faced mulla, helpless. After a few uncomfortable moments, Akbar turned again to Birbal.

"Explain yourself!" he demanded.

"Hearing is obedience, O Brightest Eminence. We could say you are 'greater than God' in one sense, because if one of your subjects displeases you, you can exile him to a land beyond your kingdom. That, clearly, God cannot do. For the farthest emptiness of the universe is His, and He is in it, and it is in Him."

The Emperor and all his court laughed. The old storyteller sighed with relief. The sour mulla gnashed his teeth.

"In time, Birbal," said the Emperor, "you may even rid my court of flatterers, which would be a bit of good fortune never before enjoyed by any King!"

The Swindling Sadhu

IN FATEHPUR SIKRI there lived a poor old Brahmin, whose fondest dream was to make the pilgrimage to the holy city of Varanasi before he died. So he saved what he could, working hard at whatever jobs came his way and humbly begging when fortune was less kind.

One day, when the winter wind sawed through the frayed cloth of his ancient shawl, he thought:

"I am old, but not yet infirm. The time to make my pilgrimage has come."

He had a problem, however. The long road to Varanasi was infested with robbers — he dared not carry all his savings with him.

"If the gods permit me to return alive," he thought, "I shall need my savings to live on. But who will guard my money for me?"

He pondered and pondered, and this delayed his journey to

Varanasi.

But one day, a holy mystic came to Fatehpur Sikri. This *sadhu*[13] did nothing but sit cross-legged under a banyan tree, thinking, visualizing, and breathing the name of the god Rama. Many people came for his blessing, offered him coins, and joined in his prayers. He was the talk of the city.

The old Brahmin tottered by one morning with his begging bowl outstretched and saw the *sadhu* sitting like an image of stone. Suddenly, the Brahmin had an idea. Going over to the *sadhu*, he said:

"Holy brother, I am bound for the city of gods, Varanasi, but I have no family to trust my savings to. But you, who care nothing for the things of this world — my money would be safe with you."

The *sadhu* suddenly came to life, spitting fire.

"How dare you speak to me of money? Don't you know *sanyasins*[14] never touch the filthy stuff? To us it is poison. If I myself have given up such baubles of the world, why should I want to look after them for you?"

The old Brahmin fell to his knees and pleaded:

"*Maharaj*, you are a holy man. You will understand my thirst for the sight of Varanasi — it is for this alone that I have come to you."

"I cannot permit myself the touch of coin," the *sadhu* replied, "but since you speak of the yearning of your soul, I will at least watch it while you are away. Dig a hole under the banyan tree, cover your markings well, and go in peace."

"Oh, thank you, thank you," cried the old Brahmin with his eyes full

[13] Holy man.
[14] Ascetic, monk.

of tears. "May heaven be your reward."

After many months, the Brahmin returned to Fatehpur Sikri, feeling ten years younger after his baptism in the River Ganges. He was glad to see the *sadhu* posing exactly as he had left him. Sitting beside the holy man, the Brahmin let a respectful silence pass before raising the subject of his money. Again, the *sadhu* seemed annoyed:

"You come straight from the holy places, and money is still on your mind. The pilgrimage has not changed you a bit. Well, go to where you buried it, and kindly take it away."

Abashed, the old Brahmin went to the banyan tree and began to dig among its roots. But he found nothing. Then he started digging in another spot. But neither was it there. The old man began to grow frantic.

"Sir, did you see anyone near that tree? My money is gone."

"I don't want to hear another word about your repulsive money!" shouted the *sadhu*. "You come here and disturb my prayers with talk of nothing but cash — next you will accuse me of stealing it — me, a holy man!"

"No," said the old beggar, "I would never say you, who have no use for worldly things, would touch my money. But I only thought — "

"Go away and never show me your face again!" shouted the *sadhu*. "And save your earthly thoughts for others."

So, shaking his head sadly, the old man wended his way.

But after a day or so, he grew so hungry from lack of money to buy even a tiny morsel, he began to think of Birbal. He was nobody, and Birbal was a great minister of state, but, still, Birbal had a reputation for helping those in trouble.

When Birbal heard the Brahmin's tale a shadow creased his brow.

"How much money was in your purse?" he asked.

"Fifty copper *paisa*," quavered the old man.

"Not much to steal for," he said. "Still, sometimes holy men are rude, but not all rude men are holy."

And Birbal gave the old Brahmin specific instructions for the next day. Then Birbal sent him to his kitchen for food and lodged him with his servants for the night.

The next day Birbal dressed himself as a simple trader, armed himself with a chest of one hundred gold pieces, and paid a visit to the cranky *sadhu*.

"Holy brother," said Birbal, kneeling, "forgive me for disturbing your meditations, but these hundred coins of flashing gold belong to my brother, who is bound for Samarkand, and I am bound there with him. He has asked me to place them in your safe care until the day, God willing, we may return."

"Gold?" said the *sadhu*, licking his lips. "I am devoted to Rama only and never touch such filth..."

"I know it offends you to hear of gold," said Birbal, "But you would be doing such a kindness if you watched our treasure so we can cross the Himalayas in peace."

"Well," said the *sadhu*, his mouth a little dry. "You know I cannot touch the stuff — but if you care to bury your gold among the roots of yonder tree..."

But just as he was speaking to Birbal, the old Brahmin returned, and, remembering Birbal's instructions to him, recited these words:

"Holy brother, remember me? I am back from Varanasi. Thank you for watching my bag of coppers. I have come to get them now."

"Friend!" said the *sadhu*, all smiles. "Welcome back! Blessings to you! Take your money — it is buried behind the *neem*[15] tree now, not under the banyan tree. I moved it so I could watch it all the better. Dig it up, dear brother, and long life."

The old Brahmin dug up his bag and found every coin intact. Winking at Birbal, he hobbled off in glee.

"Now," said the *sadhu*, turning back to Birbal and rubbing his palms, "the best place to bury that gold would be just there, where I can keep it in view." And he pointed a trembling finger at the *neem* tree ten paces away.

But hardly had he said these words than a servant from Birbal's house ran up to his master.

"Sir," said the servant, carefully repeating the message Birbal had taught him to say, "Your brother sends urgent word. The trip to Samarkand is off."

"Ah," smiled Birbal, picking up his chest of gold and bowing respectfully to the horrified *sadhu*, "then I have troubled you, holy brother, in vain."

---

[15] A tree related to mahogany with many medicinal values.

Birbal and the Crows

BIRBAL'S CLEVERNESS MADE the courtiers at Fatehpur Sikri more and more jealous of the special favor Akbar showered upon him. Almost everyone wanted to discredit him.

One day a certain court pettifogger told the Emperor that he was puzzled by a question that was truly unanswerable, probably even by Birbal. Curious, Akbar asked Birbal to try. The courtier, prepared for an easy victory, let his question fly.

"How many crows are there in Fatehpur Sikri, exactly?"

Birbal answered promptly.

"Three million, two hundred twenty thousand, seven hundred and ninety-four."

"Just a moment," said Akbar, leaning forward from the Peacock Throne. "What proof have you that there are exactly that many crows in the city?"

"If you don't believe it, O Full Moon, have this courtier of yours go out and count them. He will find exactly the number of crows I have stated."

"Yes," persisted the Great Mughal, "but suppose he finds fewer?"

"Obviously that will mean that some of the city crows have left town to visit their relatives."

"And if he discovers more?"

"In that case, their relatives from the county will have come to town to visit them."

The Thief's Stick

A RICH MERCHANT of Fatehpur Sikri presented himself at Birbal's house, complaining of the theft of ten *mohurs*[16].

"Whom do you suspect?" asked Birbal.

"To tell the truth, sir," said the merchant. "It must be one of my servants, for the money was kept in a secret place in my kitchen, and nobody could have broken in without their noticing. I have threatened them with lashes and imprisonment, but — "

"Threats do not lead to the truth," interrupted Birbal. "How many servants do you employ?"

"Seven, *Huzur*," replied the merchant.

"Make sure they are all at home tomorrow morning."

And the next day Birbal called at the merchant's splendid mansion, accompanied by a half-naked holy man, with matted hair and wild eyes. Merchant and servants alike were terrified at the sight of him.

---

[16] Mughal imperial golden coin.

"There has been a theft in this home," Birbal began gravely, "and so I have enlisted the services of this famous wizard."

With these words the magician took seven sticks of equal length from a camelhair bag, muttered a spell, and blew upon them with a crazed stare.

Handing one stick to each of the servants, Birbal said:

"By the power of this wizard, the mere touch of a thief will cause any one of these sticks to grow an inch's length overnight. Now each of you shall be locked in a separate chamber, and tomorrow we shall examine your sticks."

The servants shuddered, as each was conducted to his quarters.

When Birbal returned the following day and gathered the servants together, he told the merchant:

"Measure the stick of every man."

When he did so, he turned to Birbal in astonishment.

"*Huzur*, this is amazing — none of the sticks has grown, but the cook's is one inch shorter!"

"Then," smiled Birbal, "the cook is the thief. Only a man tormented by a guilty conscience would believe the fairy tale of magical sticks — and so he whittled his stick shorter during the night."

And so the money was recovered, the thief punished, and the fame of Birbal grew.

Neither Here Nor There

IN THE BEAUTIFUL CITY of Fatehpur Sikri, Akbar built a palace called The House of Worship. There, every Friday night, scholars, poets, and philosophers gathered from every nation in the world — even from faraway Europe. To the delight of the Emperor they discussed problems of logic and metaphysics far into the night.

One evening a dervish[16] presented himself to this august assembly and said:

"I have traveled from kingdom to kingdom, and everywhere I have defeated the wisest men in debate. Every king has given me an amulet of gold as a present, and so far I have collected forty-nine of them. When I defeat the wise men of Fatehpur Sikri, I shall win the fiftieth."

"Let us see," smiled Akbar. "Pose us a problem."

---

[16] Wandering mystic or holy man.

"My challenge is this," said the dervish:"

"Bring here before us a thing which is here but not there;

"Another which is there but not here;

"A third which is neither here nor there;

"And a fourth which is in both places."

The wise men of Akbar's court were stunned. But Birbal stepped forward and said:

"I will return in one hour."

The moon had risen above the lovely parapets of Fatehpur Sikri, when Birbal returned with three men: a thief, a *sadhu* (or holy man), and a beggar.

"Sire," Birbal began. "The dervish has asked for a thing which is here but not there. This first man is a thief. He lives on the earth among us. But he steals and cheats. He does not repent. So his prayers do not reach heaven, and neither will his soul. He is here, but not there."

And, saddened by this thought, the thief slunk away into the night.

"Next," said Birbal, "something that is there but not here. This *sadhu* does not think about this world of cares at all. He only sits and thinks about God. He is so heavenly minded, he is no earthly good. Thus, he is there but not here."

The *sadhu* stood impassive, as if he had heard not a word that had been spoken.

"Go on," said Akbar, smiling.

"This beggar is neither here nor there," said Birbal. "He does not enjoy this life, because he is poor. So he always dreams of another, better life. But he is content to beg, so he never improves his lot — he just envies those who succeed. He is neither here nor there."

The Emperor nodded sadly.

"But what about something which is both here and there?" he asked.

"This man," said Birbal. "Is none other than yourself, *Maharaj*. Even if you were not a king, you would be a generous man. He who gives all he has to others enjoys this world because those in it respect and love him. But, because he is not attached to wealth, or even to what other people think of him, but lives only to please God, his contentment will abide in the next world as well. He is both here and there."

Smiling, the dervish let all of the forty-nine amulets slip from his arms and fall ringing to the marble floor.

"Let Your Majesty rejoice," he said, "for his court is adorned with the rarest pearl of wisdom in the world."

Heaven's Gifts

"IT IS STRANGE," said Jai Mal in the Hall of Public Audience, "that Heaven should be so careless in the distribution of its blessings. One would think that God, in giving Birbal the gift of matchless wit, would have chosen somebody of noble birth or handsome features to receive it. Birbal is clever indeed, but I fear he somewhat resembles a donkey!"

There was laughter among the whole assembly, and Jai Mal preened himself at having humiliated Akbar's favorite.

The King was annoyed at such blunt rudeness, but Birbal replied:

"There is a reason for that, O Ocean of Bright Promise. Before we were born, the angels took us to the Treasure House of God and asked us to choose from among the many gifts of heaven.

"In one pavilion were stored the benefits of Wealth, and many souls gathered there, collecting as much as they could.

"In another pavilion were Beauty and Personal Charm, and other souls loaded themselves with those.

"But in a smaller pavilion, covered with cobwebs and overlooked, the riches of Intelligence were kept. I was so fascinated with these that by the time I had finished scooping them up, the other pavilions had been emptied, and our generation was delivered upon the earth.

"Now, I may have come to resemble a donkey, perhaps from living among you rich and handsome courtiers who always play the donkey's part, but at least my words ring sweetly in the Emperor's ears, even as your braying causes him to stop them up!"

And Akbar laughed, as Jai Mal gnashed his teeth.

The Egg Hunt

AKBAR'S COURTIERS were truly miserable at Birbal's success. So the Emperor decided to lift their spirits by playing his own trick on Birbal.

One day at court, he sent Birbal away on an errand. Then he had a servant bring a basket of eggs. He told the assembled grandees:

"Each of you take one egg. Later, when I tell you to dive into the garden pool, you will pretend that you each found an egg at the bottom. Understand?"

"Yes, *Jahanpanah*," said the courtiers wistfully.

"The Emperor has gone mad," they thought.

But when Birbal returned from his errand, Akbar said:

"Last night I had a dream. I dreamed I should test my courtiers to find out which of you is truly noble and which unfit to live at my court. The dream told me I should command each of you to dive into the garden pool. The worthy men would all find an egg at the bottom. But those who came up without an egg should be banished."

And the Emperor led everyone into the garden for the test. The courtiers were delighted.

"Now it is Birbal's time to look foolish," they grinned.

But Birbal noticed their whispering and thought, "Something is up."

One by one, the courtiers dived into the reflecting pond. One by one, they came up from among the water lilies holding an egg.

"Here, Your Majesty," they said, happily showing the eggs to the King. When Birbal's turn came at last, he thought, "There must be a basket of eggs at the bottom." So he unwrapped his turban and dove into the pond.

He groped through the dark water but found nothing. When his breath gave out, he burst to the surface, empty-handed.

"What?" cried Akbar angrily. "No egg?"

But instead of answering, Birbal climbed up on the wall of the tank and started to crow.

"He's lost his mind," said the courtiers. "It's the first time he's been defeated, and it's driven him crazy."

Birbal crowed again.

"What are you doing, Birbal?" asked the Emperor.

"Why, surely it's obvious," said Birbal gesturing to the soaking courtiers, each cupping an egg, "that among so many hens you will need at least one rooster!"

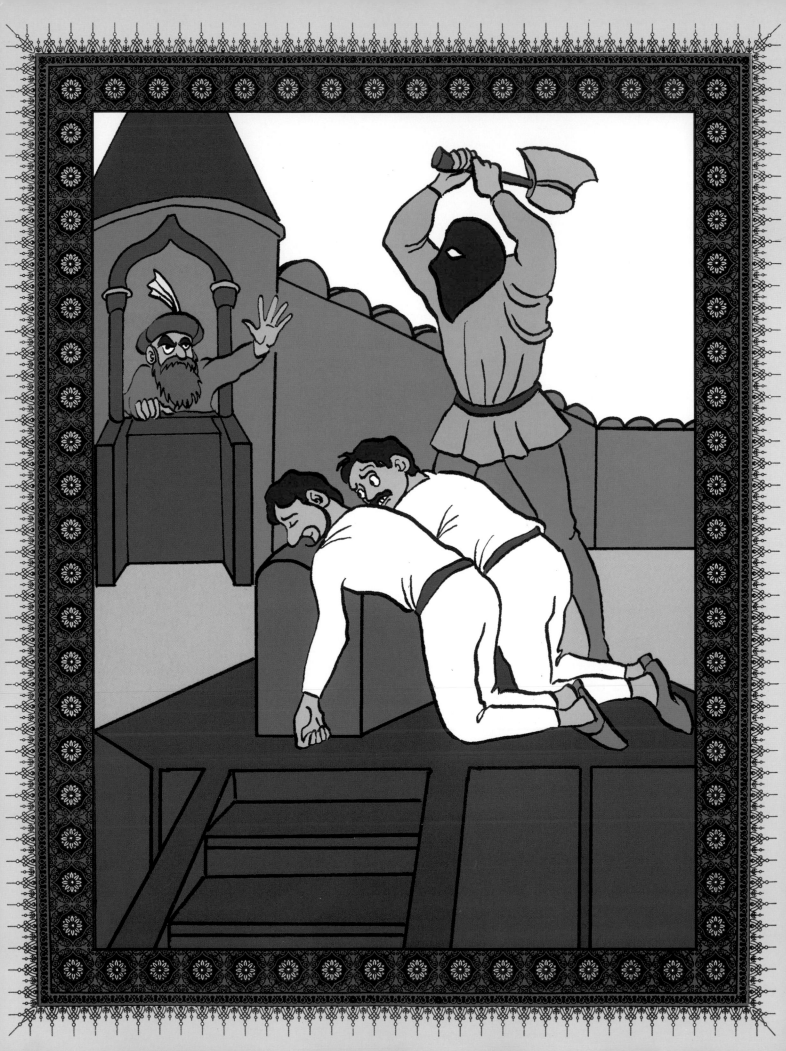

Birbal and the King of Afghanistan

JAI MAL AND THE OTHER NOBLES continued to hatch plots against the Nine Sages of Akbar's court.

Besides Birbal, one of these Nine Sages was Tansen. He was the minstrel of magical prowess. The jealous courtiers conceived a scheme to eliminate both of these upstarts at one stroke.

They told the Emperor that cleverness and talent could not overpower the irrevocable force of destiny.

"Give me an example," said Akbar.

They told him the case of a young prince, who had been sent by one king to another, bearing a secret message, which asked that the second king, as a favor to the first, put the young prince to death.

"Nobody could escape such a trap," they said. "Not Tansen. Nor even Birbal."

Nothing is more dangerous than the curiosity of kings. Akbar decided to put Tansen and Birbal to this test. He wrote to Mirza[17] Mohammed Hakim, his half-brother, the King of Afghanistan.

"Dear Brother," wrote Akbar, "the men bringing you this message are the worst criminals in my realm. Show your loyalty to me by having them killed."

Then he called Birbal and Tansen, gave them the sealed letter, and sped them on their fatal mission.

When the Afghan King read the letter, he crisped his fingers, and the messengers were thrown into the darkest dungeon. Tansen was sick with fear.

"What a miserable fate has overtaken us!" he cried. "Here we lie, condemned to die for no reason whatever."

Birbal, however, merely shrugged. When the day of execution dawned, he took Tansen by the sleeve and said:

"When the moment comes for us to die, you watch me and do everything I do."

"Oh, yes, *baba*[18]," cried Tansen, "if you think we can be saved."

They were led to the block. A huge executioner stood by, handling his shiny ax as if it itched in his palms. The King was about to give the order to chop, when Birbal cried out:

"Please, Majesty, whatever you do, kill me first!"

The King said: "If you want that, so be it. Anyway, both of you have only minutes to live."

But hardly had he finished speaking when Tansen also wailed:

[17] Prince.
[18] Father.

140

"O God's Shadow on Earth, please grant my last wish and kill me before you kill him!"

And both of them pleaded and made such a noise that the King had to shout for silence.

"Both of you are on the brink of Eternal Night," he thundered. "What possible difference does it make which of you the ax cleaves last?"

Neither prisoner spoke. Great beads of sweat ran down Tansen's neck.

"Listen," said the King, "whichever of you explains why he wants to die first, I will kill him before the other."

Tansen looked at Birbal in bewilderment. Birbal at last spoke up.

"You see, Highness," he murmured, "it is a matter of astrology."

"Astrology?" sneered the King.

"Yes, Sire," said Birbal. "According to the stars, whoever is executed in Kabul — just at this precise moment — will come back in his next life as Conqueror of Afghanistan."

"What!" The King rose from his throne.

"Yes, Sire," said Birbal. "Now please, since I have told you the secret, give your Crown to me in my next life. Let me die first."

When the King heard these words, he glared first at one ragged prisoner, then at the other. Rubbing his huge beard, he thought, "This is Akbar's trick to take over my kingdom without a war."

And clapping his hands, he ordered:

"Execution indefinitely postponed."

Birbal's Journey to Paradise

THE COURT BARBER NURSED his hatred for Birbal and plotted daily against him. Finally, he hit on a plan. When the Emperor Akbar next called him to trim his beard, he said:

"You know, *Jahanpanah*, last night I dreamed about your father."

The Great Mughal at once took interest.

"Tell me what he said to you."

"He is very happy in Paradise, but he says that all the inhabitants of Heaven are terrible bores. He would like you to send him someone who can talk to him and keep him amused."

Of course no one possessed a wit like Birbal's, and, although Akbar prized him very much, to appease his poor father in Paradise, he would consent to give Birbal up. Naturally, the only way of reaching Heaven is through death.

When Birbal responded to the Emperor's summons, Akbar said:

"I think you love me, Birbal, enough to make any sacrifice for my sake."

"You know I do, *Jahanpanah*."

"Then I would like you to go to Heaven and keep my dear father company."

"Very well," Birbal said evenly, "but please give me a few days to prepare."

"Certainly," said the King, delighted. "You are doing me a great favor. I will give you a week."

Birbal went home and dug a deep pit, which would serve as his own grave. But he also excavated a secret tunnel that opened under the floor of his house. Then he returned to the Imperial Court.

"*Maharaj*," he said, "in accordance with an old family tradition, I would like to be buried near my house — and, if you don't mind, I would like to be buried alive. I have heard that is a less painful way to die."

So, to the great happiness of the court barber, Birbal was buried alive. Of course, Birbal made his way at once through the tunnel into his own house, where he stayed in hiding for six months, neither going out in the sun nor touching a razor.

At the end of that time, with his hair and beard grown long and shaggy, he came out of hiding and obtained an audience with the Great Mughal.

"Birbal!" cried the Emperor. "Where have you come from?"

"From Paradise, Majesty. I spent such a lovely time with your father that he asked God to give me special permission to return to earth."

Akbar was astounded.

"But this is a miracle!" he cried. "Did the old Emperor give you any message for me?"

"Just one, O Peacock of the Age. Do you see my shaggy whiskers and long hair? Well, it seems very few barbers make it to Heaven. Your father asks you to send him yours at once."

The Legend of Birbal Endures

SO BIRBAL SERVED AKBAR, and Akbar served the people of India for many years. As the tales of these two clever and compassionate men were told from the frozen Hindu Kush to the palm-lined shores of Bengal while they lived, they continue to be told, as a delight for children and a lesson for adults, down to the present day.

The Real Akbar

BIRBAL AND AKBAR are surely some of the best-loved figures in the folklore of India. For generations their stories have delighted children and grown-ups alike, from one end of India to the other.

Jalaludin Mohammed Akbar Padshah Ghazi, Emperor of Hindustan, ruled from 1560 to 1605. Akbar was great in an age of great rulers: Elizabeth I of England, Henry IV of France, Philip II of Spain, Sulaiman the Magnificent of Turkey, and Shah Abbas the Great of Persia.

Akbar was chivalrous and just to all men, but he could be violent and overmastering, if needed. His magnetic personality won the love and affection of his people and the respect and admiration of his enemies.

Akbar was superb at riding, polo and swordsmanship, and he was a crack shot with a musket. He was courageous, often fighting personally in the heat of battle. He was a brilliant general, a master of speed, surprise, and logistics. His lightening conquests of India, from the Hindu Kush to Bengal, were feats of military genius.

Akbar worked hard at the trade of king, sleeping only three hours a night. Although he could neither read nor write (he was probably dyslexic), he had legions of scholars who read to him. His son, Prince Sultan Salim, later the Emperor Jahangir, wrote that from his great learning no one could have guessed that Akbar was illiterate. He loved religion, philosophy, music, architecture, poetry, history and painting. He forged an Empire that enjoyed long-lasting peace and high cultural refinement.

The Empire of the Mughals was vast and fabulously rich. Akbar's lower taxes and rising conquests created prosperity for the people and floods of treasure for the Crown. European visitors estimated that just one province of Akbar's Empire, Bengal, was wealthier than France and England combined.

HISTORICAL NOTE:
The Real Birbal

BIRBAL WAS BORN TO a poor Brahmin family of Tikawanpur on the banks of the River Jumna. He rose to the exalted level of minister (or "Raja") at Akbar's court by virtue of his razorlike wit. He was a good poet, writing under the pen name "Brahma," and a collection of his verse is preserved today in the Bharatpur Museum.

Birbal's duties at court were administrative and military, but his close friendship with the Emperor was sealed by Akbar's love of wisdom and subtle humor. In Birbal the young King found a true sympathizer and companion. When, in an attempt to unify his Hindu and Muslim subjects, Akbar founded a new religion of universal tolerance, the *Din-I-Ilahi*, or "Divine Faith," there was only one Hindu among the handful of his followers, and that was Birbal.

Many courtiers were jealous of Birbal's starlike rise to fortune and power, and, according to popular accounts, they were endlessly plotting his downfall.

The character of Akbar in these stories is rather fanciful, and, historically, Birbal is scarcely heard of. Many of these tales were probably invented by village storytellers over the ages and simply attributed to Birbal and Akbar because their characters seemed to fit.

Akbar's court was mobile, a tradition handed down from his nomadic ancestors, the Mongols of Central Asia. (Mughal is Urdu for Mongol.) The Emperor ruled sometimes from the fortress of Agra, sometimes from the noble city of Lahore. In the period of these tales, 1571 to 1585, Akbar held court in the shimmering pleasure city that he had built for himself — Fatehpur Sikri.

Birbal's beautiful home may still be seen in the abandoned city of Fatehpur Sikri, near Agra. This domed, two-story house is a lovely example of structural and decorative harmony in a residence of Mughal times.

The End of Birbal

BIRBAL WAS KILLED in battle when he was leading a difficult expedition against the Afghans in 1586. Rumors spread that his fall was due to treachery. Perhaps the jealous courtiers had at last had their revenge.

When Akbar learned of Birbal's death, he took no food for two days and two nights. Overwhelmed with grief, the King blurted out this lament:

> O Birbal,
> To the helpless you never brought harm.
> You gave them all that you had.
> O friend, who will be my right arm,
> Now that I am left helpless and sad?

Summerwind Marketing, Inc.

PO Box 60013

Pasadena CA 91116-6013 USA

(888) 820-8140

(888) 820-8140 FAX

jimmoseley@wwdb.org

www.birbal.net

Summerwind Marketing
Quick Order Form

- Fax orders: (888) 820-8140. Send this form
- Telephone orders: (888) 820-8140. Have your credit card ready.
- Email orders: http://www.birbal.net/order_your_copy.htm.
- Postal orders: Summerwind Marketing, Inc.,
  PO Box 60013, Pasadena CA 91116-6013, USA. (888) 820-8140.

Please send me the following items. I understand that I may return any of them for a full refund, for any reason, no questions asked.

☐ **The Ninth Jewel of the Mughal Crown:**
The Birbal Tales from the Oral Traditions of India, Volume 1
$24.95 x Qty _____ = Total _____

☐ **A Caravan from Hindustan:**
The Birbal Tales from the Oral Traditions of India, Volume 2
Coming Soon

☐ **A Companion to the King:**
The Birbal Tales from the Oral Traditions of India, Volume 3
Coming Soon

☐ Other _____

☐ Please put me on a notification list for volumes 2 and 3 of The Birbal Tales and other future titles from Summerwind.

Name: _____

Address: _____

City: _____ State: _____ ZIP Code: _____

Telephone: (_____) _____ e-mail address: _____

Shipping by air:

US: $4 for the first product and $2.00 for each additional product.

International: $9 for the first product and $5 for each additional product.

Payment:
☐ Check
☐ Credit Card:
☐ Visa   ☐ MasterCard   ☐ American Express   ☐ Discover   ☐ Optima
Card Number: _____
Name on card: _____ Exp. Date:_____/_____

Summerwind Marketing, Inc.

PO Box 60013

Pasadena CA 91116-6013 USA

(888) 820-8140

(888) 820-8140 FAX

jimmoseley@wwdb.org

www.birbal.net

Summerwind Marketing
Quick Order Form

- Fax orders: (888) 820-8140. Send this form
- Telephone orders: (888) 820-8140. Have your credit card ready.
- Email orders: http://www.birbal.net/order_your_copy.htm.
- Postal orders: Summerwind Marketing, Inc.,
  PO Box 60013, Pasadena CA 91116-6013, USA. (888) 820-8140.

Please send me the following items. I understand that I may return any of them for a full refund, for any reason, no questions asked.

☐ **The Ninth Jewel of the Mughal Crown:**
The Birbal Tales from the Oral Traditions of India, Volume 1

$24.95 x Qty _____ = Total _____

☐ **A Caravan from Hindustan:**
The Birbal Tales from the Oral Traditions of India, Volume 2

Coming Soon

☐ **A Companion to the King:**
The Birbal Tales from the Oral Traditions of India, Volume 3

Coming Soon

☐ Other _____

☐ Please put me on a notification list for volumes 2 and 3 of The Birbal Tales and other future titles from Summerwind.

Name: _____

Address: _____

City: _____ State: _____ ZIP Code: _____

Telephone: (_____) _____ e-mail address: _____

Shipping by air:

US: $4 for the first product and $2.00 for each additional product.

International: $9 for the first product and $5 for each additional product.

Payment:

☐ Check

☐ Credit Card:

☐ Visa   ☐ MasterCard   ☐ American Express   ☐ Discover   ☐ Optima

Card Number: _____

Name on card: _____ Exp. Date:____/_____

Summerwind Marketing, Inc.

PO Box 60013

Pasadena CA 91116-6013 USA

(888) 820-8140

(888) 820-8140 FAX

jimmoseley@wwdb.org

www.birbal.net

Summerwind Marketing
Quick Order Form

- Fax orders: (888) 820-8140. Send this form
- Telephone orders: (888) 820-8140. Have your credit card ready.
- Email orders: http://www.birbal.net/order_your_copy.htm.
- Postal orders: Summerwind Marketing, Inc.,
  PO Box 60013, Pasadena CA 91116-6013, USA. (888) 820-8140.

Please send me the following items. I understand that I may return any of them for a full refund, for any reason, no questions asked.

☐ **The Ninth Jewel of the Mughal Crown:**
The Birbal Tales from the Oral Traditions of India, Volume 1

$24.95 x Qty _____ = Total _____

☐ **A Caravan from Hindustan:**
The Birbal Tales from the Oral Traditions of India, Volume 2

Coming Soon

☐ **A Companion to the King:**
The Birbal Tales from the Oral Traditions of India, Volume 3

Coming Soon

☐ Other _____

☐ Please put me on a notification list for volumes 2 and 3 of The Birbal Tales and other future titles from Summerwind.

Name: _____

Address: _____

City: _____ State: _____ ZIP Code: _____

Telephone: (_____) _____ e-mail address: _____

Shipping by air:

US: $4 for the first product and $2.00 for each additional product.

International: $9 for the first product and $5 for each additional product.

Payment:

☐ Check

☐ Credit Card:

☐ Visa   ☐ MasterCard   ☐ American Express   ☐ Discover   ☐ Optima

Card Number: _____

Name on card: _____ Exp. Date: _____/_____